Vengeance Unbound

There are some who brand Russell Dane a coward and some believe he is a murderer. The man he should have fought in a duel wants him dead as does his Uncle Clive. As if that were not enough the town that tried to lynch him wants him dead and the outlaws he takes refuge with also want him dead.

With so many out for his blood Russell Dane has only one option. He has to learn to handle a Colt. He must confront all his enemies before he can find peace.

Is his gun craft enough to keep him alive?

Vengeance Unbound

Henry Christopher

A Black Horse Western

ROBERT HALE · LONDON

ISBN 978-0-7090-8376-4

Robert Hale Limited
Clerkenwell House
Clerkenwell Green
London EC1R 0HT

Typeset by
Derek Doyle & Associates, Shaw Heath
Printed and bound in Great Britain by
Antony Rowe Limited, Wiltshire

1

'You think he'll turn up?'

'If he is to keep his place in the academy he has to turn up no matter what.'

Leonard Forten was an elegantly dressed young man whose father had been a senator. Leonard had inherited the family wealth when his father was killed in a shootout with another senator, from Missouri, named Charlie Dane. A jury had acquitted Dane of the charge of murder. Forten it was who had called out Dane and then drew first, only to be gunned down by the man he challenged. After the trial Dane had resigned his position of senator and retired to his ranch in Missouri.

Forten and his companions were students at the Virginia Military Academy – all young men and all from wealthy families. Now they stood in a clearing in Treakson Wood and waited. There was a certain air of apprehension amongst the young men. Just visible through the trees down on the road could be seen a carriage parked off the road.

It was early morning and a chill wind stirred the branches of the wood. In the distance came the sound of another carriage and the young men visibly tensed. They peered in the direction from which came the clatter of hoofs and the rumble of wheels. Instinctively they grouped closer together and watched as the second carriage drew up. They could hear the driver calling to the team to halt. Two men alighted from the vehicle and came hurrying through the trees.

'Is it Dane?' Forten asked of his companions.

The young men were craning their necks and angling their gaze in an attempt to identify the approaching men.

'Damnit, I think not. It's Pierce with Doctor Owen.'

They watched as the two men entered the clearing – one a handsomely dressed youngster like themselves and the second an older man in a broadcloth suit.

The younger of the newcomers smiled at the men gathered in the clearing. He carried a flat, polished wood box under his arm.

'*Voila, mon ami.* I have brought the good doctor and the duelling pistols.'

He cocked his head to one side as he took in the small group of men.

'But where is Monsieur Dane? He has not arrived?'

'Ahem.'

The slight clearing of his throat by the older man caught their attention.

'It seems I was brought here under false pretences,' the doctor observed mildly. 'Monsieur Morais asked me to accompany him here fearing that someone had been seriously wounded. He brings with him duelling pistols. I take it I am to be witness to a duel? The serious wounding has yet to occur.'

'Forgive me, Monsieur Doctor, I could think of no other way to get you out here.'

'Very well, can I persuade you boys to abandon this foolishness, shake hands and go back to the college and eat a hearty breakfast?'

Leonard Forten stepped forward.

'I apologize for this deception, Doctor. I am committed to this course of action and nothing you can say will change my mind. It is a question of honour.'

The doctor nodded wisely.

'Ah yes, honour, what else!'

He looked towards the young man's companions.

'Who is it that you have this issue of honour with?'

'My quarrel is with Russell Dane. He has not arrived in the field yet.'

The doctor pursed his lips and stared thoughtfully at the young man standing so sure and upright before him.

'In that case my services will not be required.'

He turned to the young Frenchman who had brought him to the duelling place.

'Monsieur Morais, would you be so kind as to allow me use of your carriage to take me back to town.'

Before Morais could reply Leonard Forten stepped forward and gripped the doctor by the arm.

'What the hell do you mean, your services will not be required?' he hissed.

The doctor looked pointedly down at the hand gripping his elbow. Reluctantly the youngster released him.

'Russell Dane was called back home early this morning. He received a message late last night telling of the sudden death of his father. He left immediately. If you wish to continue your quarrel with him you will have to follow him to his home.'

For a moment Forten stared at the doctor.

'If this is true . . .' His words trailed off. 'The Danes and my family have been feuding for years. In one way this is good news that Charles Dane is dead, for he murdered my father. But it appears to rob me of the opportunity to

7

avenge the murder and kill his son, Russell.'

He blinked a number of times while staring at the doctor before turning back to his companions.

'How convenient. I had my doubts he would face me like a man. It looks as if I shall have to kill him another day. Come my friends, we shall do as the good doctor suggests and return to a hearty breakfast. The coward Russell Dane lives to run away another day.'

Russell Dane stared out through the carriage window as his train rattled and clanged across the countryside. At that point in his journey back to his home the train was labouring up a steep slope as it threaded its way through the Allegheny mountain range. Though Russell stared out at the tree-covered slopes, he was not aware of the stands of spruce and pine and laurel as they passed in endless panorama before his unseeing eyes.

The telegram had come with its brief but shocking summons.

COME HOME. FATHER IN FATAL ACCIDENT. MOTHER.

Everything else had faded into insignificance with the words of that message seared in his brain. *Father in fatal accident.*

He was still numb with the shock of it. Without a thought to say goodbye to any of his friends, he had immediately walked out of the academy buildings and booked his passage home. It was too soon for grief. He was still in a state of denial. There had been a terrible mistake.

Perhaps there had been a slip-up over the wording of the message. The operator had substituted fatal for serious. That was it – serious accident – not fatal accident. His father had a serious accident.

That big, gruff man could not be dead. There was too much life in that great bull of a man. Senator Dane had dominated the young Russell's life for as long as he could remember.

For a brief time his father had neglected his family to travel to the Capitol to carry out duties as a senator. For Russell, that had been a miserable time. He was very young at the time and could not understand why his father had deserted his family. Many a night he had cried himself to sleep, inconsolable in his grief.

His father's brief visits were not enough to compensate the young boy for the long days without his hero. Then had come the scandal over the gunfight. Senators did not indulge in gunplay especially when another senator dies as a result.

Too young to understand the implications of what had occurred, young Russell had been ecstatic when his father had returned to the family ranch for good. From then on his father had devoted himself to ranching and as a result the business had prospered.

The ex-senator had acquired a golden touch. He bought up land around him at a phenomenal rate, increasing his range to build up one of the largest and most prosperous ranches in the state of Missouri. It was inconceivable that such a man was dead.

With a sigh, Russell Dane sat back in his seat and stared up at the ceiling of the railcar. Suddenly he sat bolt upright again.

'The duel,' he said aloud. 'I was to fight Leonard Forten.'

He sat there, his mind in turmoil. As he stared unseeingly before him, slowly the rhythm of the clacking wheels carrying him home began to drive words into his brain.

The coward runs – father is dead.

The coward runs – father is dead.

He clenched his fists and shook his head trying to block out the brutal rhyme. But the mocking refrain was not to be denied. The metal wheels throbbed on and on.

The coward runs – father is dead.

2

Elsinburg Cemetery was ancient, as was evident from the weathered headboards and headstones. The Dane plot held a place of prominence on the hill overlooking the rows of graves, as was fitting for the most important family in the county. A fine stone sarcophagus had been erected with carved figures of soldiers carrying arms into war, evidence of the warrior culture of the Dane family.

The Dane mausoleum could be seen from the town and, indeed, travellers on the road to and from Elsinburg had to ride almost in the shadow of that eminent structure.

Danes had fought against the British in the War of Independence and were depicted by a buckskin-clad figure parrying the thrust of an English bayonet. Another carving showed a Spanish soldier falling under the flintlock of an American soldier during the Mexican war. Carved Apaches attacked a covered wagon. The most recent War of the States was one in which the man now being interred had fought, and remembrance of that conflict was still to be decided.

The graveyard was crowded this day with the living. People could be seen threading their way amongst the graves. As they drew near the Dane tomb, the sobbing of a woman could be heard mingled with the murmur of the crowd of onlookers.

Mrs Gertrude Dane, dressed entirely in black with veiled face, sobbed unceasingly as she stood by the vault. The coffin containing the remains of her late husband rested on wooden supports awaiting entombment. By her side stood her son Russell and on the other side was his uncle, Clive Dane.

The ceremony over, Clive escorted the grieving widow to the carriage waiting on the road below. The onlookers were filing out of the graveyard, some climbing onto horses or vehicles parked on the road while others began the short walk back into town. As the graveyard emptied, one lonely figure remained standing by the Dane vault.

Russell Dane stared with tragic eyes at the last resting place of his father. His face was pale and his eyes ringed with dark smudges, evidence of disturbed nights. It was an intelligent face with deep thoughtful eyes and overhanging brow. A soft well-groomed beard covered the lower half of his face.

'Father, dear father, why did you have to leave me now? My mind is troubled with what I have left behind at the academy. You were brave and wise. I am in need of your guidance. I must go back and face Leonard Forten. You slew his father and his son wants to take out his revenge on me. Now that I have lost a father, I understand better his feelings of loss. I do not want to fight him. Do you think I am a coward for not wanting to fight?'

Slowly he leaned forward and rested his hands on the iron rails that cordoned off the ornate vault. The noise of vehicles faded into the distance and Russell was alone with his grief. So wrapped up was he in his self-pity he did not notice the three riders pull up on the road and dismount. They tied up their horses and began to clamber up towards the lonely figure in the graveyard.

At last he heard the men approaching. He turned and frowned at the threesome. They were young men dressed in Sunday best. They had left on the riding boots and spurs – necessary accessories for every working cowboy.

'Russell, goddamn it, stop mooning about up here and come into town with us and we'll help you drown your sorrows.'

'Bernard, by all that's holy, why are you troubling me at such a time?' Russell looked askance at Bernard's two brothers flanking him. 'And you, Mathew and Francis, you should know better.'

The brothers gathered round the young Russell unabashed by his surly greeting.

'Come Russell, we cannot have you moping here all alone. Madam Red Eye is calling. She says, imbibe with me and I will help you forget your sorrows.'

'We won't take no for an answer. If we have to, we'll hogtie you and carry you down to the town and pour bourbon into you till you are insensible. Since you went away to the academy the girls at the Cosmopolitan have been distraught. They pester us penniless cowboys for news of their favourite boy. You broke their hearts when you went away. They pine for your attention, Russell. Do not deny them a night of bliss in your company.'

'Boys, I'm not in the mood. Can't you see that? My father lies dead in this tomb. Leave me to my sorrow.'

'Right fellas, it looks as if we have to take him by force. You, Russell, are coming down to the Cosmopolitan Saloon if we have to drag you kicking and screaming down there.'

His friends surrounded him with determined expressions on their faces. For a moment Russell tried to look annoyed, but he could not be angry with the brothers for long. He threw up his hands in surrender and allowed them to escort him down to the road where he rode double with Bernard as they turned their horses round and headed back to town.

3

The Cosmopolitan Saloon was crowded and the four friends had to push through a throng of drinkers to get to the bar. They ordered a bottle of bourbon and four schooners of beer from the busy barmen. Then they huddled together against the encroaching swarm of drinkers, some the worse for wear and carousing rowdily.

'What are your plans now, Russell?'

'I guess I'll go back to the academy and continue my studies.'

The suggestion brought with it the memory of what he had escaped when he was suddenly called home.

Forten and he had quarrelled. The row was long overdue for Forten went out of his way to be obnoxious to the younger student. At every opportunity he had made his enmity obvious. Russell was well aware of the reason for the older student's dislike. In fact it was more than dislike – it was out-and-out hatred.

The fact that Russell's father had killed the elder Forten in a shootout was reason enough for that hatred. Then had come the challenge. Forten had made sure it was done in the most public manner. Russell had no option but to accept. Then had come the message from his mother telling him his father was dead.

'Goddamn it if it ain't the milksop, Dane. . . .'

Russell's introspection was interrupted by the rough voice bawling out this observation. He looked up and saw a face from the past. Harry Roach, for reasons unfathomable, hated Russell Dane. Perhaps it was because Russell was everything Roach was not. The Danes were a family of wealth and influence. They owned the biggest spread in the territory. Russell was handsome and intelligent.

Harry Roach came from a family of dirt-poor farmers. His father was a drunk and a thief. Harry was following in his father's footsteps. Right now he was three parts drunk and his old antagonist had surfaced in the Cosmopolitan Saloon. Roach was in an ugly mood and looking for trouble. He swayed before the youngsters and leered at Russell.

'I hear your pa died sudden. Well it weren't sudden enough. You can't hide behind your big shot senator pa no more. I'm gonna thrash you. I shoulda done it long ago.'

Roach licked his thin lips. His oval face was an unhealthy pallor. Unpleasantly ugly, he peered through narrow squinting eyes. He was a couple of years older than the four friends. At school he had been a dunce. This had caused an intense jealousy of Russell who always came first in any subject and was much admired and praised by his teachers.

'I hear they run you outta that academy for cowardice, Dane. Well, you can't run anywhere now.'

With these words Roach lurched towards Russell. Bernard, lean and dangerous, stepped in front of the drunk.

'Damnit, Harry, leave the kid alone. Christ, his pa's just died. Have you no feelings?'

Roach immediately butted Bernard in the face, driving him back into Russell's arms. Russell staggered back losing his drink as he tried to hold on to his friend. Bernard's nose streamed blood.

Francis was the younger of the brothers but was going bald and this made him look older than his siblings. As if to add to the impression of maturity, Francis was trying to grow a small goatee beard which showed up as grubby streaks on his face. He swung a wild punch that hit the drunkard in the jaw.

Roach cursed and went for his sidearm. He managed to get his pistol out but before he could bring it up level to start shooting, Bernard drove his boot hard into the gunman's midriff. At the same time his brother, Mathew, a slim cowboy with dirty blonde hair, smashed his tankard on to the drunkard's wrist. The glass shattered, splashing beer far and wide. With a yelp, Roach lost his grip on the weapon and lurched back into the safety of the crowd.

This was the point Roach's companions decided to take a hand. Tyrone Deffy, a bruiser of a man, threw himself into the mêlée. He crashed into the pals and they went down in a tangle of legs and arms. The only one left standing was Russell. He brought his knee up into the bruiser's face as he grappled with Bernard. A fist came from nowhere and smashed Russell in the jaw. As he went down a boot caught him in the ribs.

'Goddamn it,' he muttered, as he struggled to rise amidst a forest of boots trying to trample him back into the sawdust. 'I only came in for a quiet drink.'

He was on his feet again, punching and kicking at anyone that came near. Alcohol and excited movement are precursors to violence. The fight spread as men lunged forward, eager to see what was happening, and were drawn into the fracas. In a very short time a mini riot was in progress.

The bartenders looked in disbelief as the brawling extended into the gambling area. The girls working the tables were screaming and trying to get out of harm's way. A whistle shrilled and the bartenders leapt into the fray. They were armed with thick wooden clubs.

Slowly they worked through the brawling crowd. They flailed about them mercilessly. Men were indiscriminately bludgeoned insensible. The bartender brigade worked tirelessly at the beating. It was steady and effective. Within a short time they had laid out enough of the fighters to dampen down the excitement. The survivors were scrambling to get away from the baton-wielding barkeeps. Eventually order was restored and a relative calm returned to the Cosmopolitan.

Russell had escaped onto the stairs, narrowly escaping the punishment meted out by the bruising barmen. He felt a hand on his shoulder and nervously whirled about, tensing for a blow. A young woman was sitting on the steps above him, smiling down at him.

'Russell, you have decided to come back to us.' Her voice was soft and warm. 'We did miss our favourite fella.'

For a few moments he stared at the girl. She had a full, wide mouth and a mass of dark curls. Her eyes were wide-set, dark and deep, and she was staring soulfully at Russell.

'Ophelia, as I live and breathe, it is Ophelia.'

'Come upstairs with me, Russell. Let's get reacquainted.'

'We had some good times together, Ophelia.'

Russell looked back down into the saloon. He could not

16

immediately see his pals in the crowded bar room.

'Hell, why not! Can you get a bottle?'

She grinned mischievously at him. 'I got a good bourbon in my room. Been saving it for a special occasion. I reckon as this is it.'

Russell rose to his feet and grabbed the girl's hand.

'Let's do it.'

4

'Oh my aching head,' Russell groaned as he awoke to full consciousness.

He stared at the discoloured ceiling and idly watched the insects teeming across the surface with alarming energy. He closed his eyes and the insects continued to swarm inside his eyelids. At last he opened his eyes and turned his gaze to a misshapen lump in the bed beside him. For a moment he stared at this in some puzzlement.

'Where the hell am I?'

There was a grunt from inside the bed covers and the whole thing moved. He watched with detached interest as a tousled head emerged and a girl blinked owlishly before focusing her gaze on him.

'Howdy,' he said.

'Russell, what the hell time is it?'

He thought about this for a moment.

'Must be morning.'

'What day is it?'

'No idea. How long have I been here?'

'I guess a couple of days,' she answered.

He covered his eyes with his hands.

'I got flies swarming all over my eyeballs.'

She suddenly started giggling.

'What's so goddamn funny?'

'I guess that's why it's called redeye. Your eyes look like fried eggs.'

He groaned. 'I gotta get myself a drink.'

He tried to rouse himself from the bed and fell back with another groan.

'I ain't never gonna touch another drink in my whole goddamn life.'

The girl reached out of the bed and felt around on the floor. She came up with a partially filled bourbon bottle and swished the contents around.

'There's enough here for a couple of swigs.'

'Here, gimme.'

He reached across and took the bottle from her. For a moment he contemplated the amber liquor.

'Here's to good old goddamn likker. The pathway to oblivion.'

Carefully he placed the neck of the bottle to his lips and tilted it. There was a gurgling sound as he drank. He left off drinking and looked questioningly at the girl in the bed beside him.

'You wanna swig of this goddamn medicine?'

She shook her head.

'I ain't got the stomach for it no more.'

He finished the residue in the bottle and sombrely regarded the empty vessel.

'Another dead man,' he pronounced gloomily.

The girl reached over and placed her hand on Russell's shoulder.

'Russell, I guess I never rightly said as how I was sorry about your pa's death. All us girls were sure broke up about it. He was a fine man. Allus treated us girls at the Cosmopolitan with respect. How's your ma taking it?'

Russell sat up suddenly and immediately regretted the abrupt movement.

'Goddamn it, my head's spinning like a mule on locoweed. I was supposed to go out to the ranch with Mother. Then Bernard and his friends hijacked me.' He frowned. 'Was there a fight or something? I seem to remember something about a brawl.'

The girl beside him yawned prodigiously.

'Russell Dane, you are the limit,' she said indistinctly through her wide-open mouth, and continued yawning. 'Harry Roach and company set upon you lot but got more than they bargained for. Your friends kicked the living daylights outta them. Then the barkeeps busted some skulls and the place settled down after that'

'I gotta go and see Ma. I been all jumbled since I got back with the arrangements for the funeral and all. She was in a bad way over Pa's death. Me too for that matter.'

'Russell, I am sorry.'

She watched him ease out onto the floor and search for his clothes. Then she snuggled back down into the bed.

'When will I see you again, Russell?' she asked sleepily.

'Where's my goddamn boots?'

Russell hired a hack from the livery and started out on the ride to the family ranch. By the time he reached the ranch his head was pounding worse than when he woke that afternoon. The sun was low in the sky and the settling gloom of the evening suited his pessimistic mood. Now that his father was gone it seemed there was no joy left in life. Try as he might, he could not shrug off the heavy sadness that seemed to overwhelm him.

As he approached the extensive buildings that made up the ranch he noticed the traps and gigs and saddle-ponies tethered around the yard.

'I guess the mourning process is still going on,' he mused.

He was not looking forward to meeting the neighbours and friends that would have come to the ranch to sympathize with his mother in her grief. For a brief moment he was tempted to head for the bunkhouse and search out his cowboy companions.

'Bernard and the boys will have a bottle stashed away, I'm sure.' But on reflection he decided he had stayed away long enough. 'Hell, I'd better go on in and show my face,' he grumbled.

To postpone the moment of entry, he took some time rubbing down his hired horse. When he finished these tasks he turned it into the corral along with the other mounts quietly browsing within the enclosure. Reluctantly he turned his feet towards the house.

The inside of the large rambling house was crowded with people. Most were middle-aged and dressed in their best finery. Russell slunk inside and tried to blend in without attracting attention. Indeed no one took much notice of the youngster as he eased along the corridor and peered through the crowd into the front parlour.

The room was spacious with a high ceiling. The walls were decorated with the accoutrements of the history of the Dane family. Battle flags, weapons and portraits of men in uniform were hung around the room giving it the atmosphere of a museum instead of a family home. Most of the guests held drinks and they were staring attentively towards the huge stone fireplace. No fire had been lit for it was late in the summer; the evenings were still mild.

Russell scouted the room to locate the whereabouts of the drinks. A couple of young girls dressed in maids' uniforms were circulating with trays. Securing a glass from one of the trays, Russell sniffed the dark-looking contents.

'Goddamn wine,' he muttered disparagingly.

He tossed back the contents in one swig and grabbed another two glasses. Then he caught sight of his mother at the same time as she noticed him. She was standing by the large fireplace and beckoning to him. He chose to pretend she was waving a greeting, and waved back. At the same time he saw his uncle standing near his mother.

5

Clive Dane stood beside his dead brother's widow and looked as if he had made himself at home in the Dane household. Russell stared with some unease at his uncle. It did not seem right that it was his Uncle Clive and not his father standing up there holding court amongst the guests. Covertly he studied the man.

His father's brother was a large-framed man with a bulky body now running to fat. His fleshy face was dominated by an overgenerous nose that contrasted with his thin mean-looking mouth. He affected a close-cropped greyish beard.

His big hand dwarfed a full whiskey glass as he gazed around the crowded room with the contented look of a man who had achieved his objective in life – a man who was entirely at home.

As Russell watched, his uncle motioned towards his

brother's widow. Gertrude Dane turned and smiled at her brother-in-law. The youngster shrank farther back against the rear wall hoping no one had noticed him as he glowered across the room at his uncle.

'Friends, listen up a while,' his uncle called to the assembly. 'I have an important announcement to make.'

Heads turned towards the speaker and the hum of conversation slowly died.

'I would like to thank you all for coming to the funeral. The sad occasion was made more bearable by the presence of so many good friends and neighbours. My brother was well liked and respected in this county. He would have been proud to see so many of his friends here tonight. On behalf of the Dane family I must thank you all for your support during this difficult time.'

The big man turned and his hand reached out and took the widow's hand in his. She smiled wanly at him.

'This is more than a get-together to say farewell to a great man who achieved so much in his lifetime. As well as a tribute to my brother, it is also a cause for celebration. I have asked Gertrude to be my wife and to my great delight she has consented. When a proper time has lapsed we will be wed in Elsinburg church early next month.'

There were a few gasps from among the assembled guests that carried to Russell's listening ears. He was leaning against the wall staring with uneasy eyes at the happy couple at the other side of the room.

Smiling brightly, Gertrude Dane turned and made her way through the crowd of guests. She was heading for her son at the back of the room.

'Russell, come and join us. Are you all right? You look a mite peaky.' She put out a hand to him. 'I know the death of your father has hit you hard as it has me, being so sudden, but life must go on.'

Russell noticed his uncle heading over to them. 'Here comes your husband-to-be, Mother. This is a bit sudden, isn't it?'

'Russell, I know what it must seem, coming so soon after your dear father's death. I . . . I need someone to run the ranch. When I offered the job to Clive it was he who suggested we cement our relationship in a more permanent manner. He's a strong man and he'll keep the ranch going till you come of age.'

'Till I come of age, Mother, till I come of age. . . .'

'Russell.'

Clive Dane put out a large hand for his nephew to shake. When the youngster ignored it he smiled indulgently and instead clapped Russell on the shoulder.

'Why so glum, nephew – or should I call you son, now that Gertrude and I are to tie the knot and I am to become your father, so to say?'

'I mourn my father,' Russell replied, putting emphasis on the word father.

'Russell, Russell, your father would not have approved of this long face. He was full of fun and, from what I remember of him, enjoyed a party. So put off this glum look and enjoy the celebration. I'm reminded of a Shakespeare quote. "I come to bury Caesar not to praise him". Well, I would say instead, I come to bury Charlie and to celebrate his life. And what better way of celebrating than a wedding? Your father would have wanted me to look after his family and, as I have no other ties, what better way of doing that than Gertrude, you and me living together under the one roof in harmony.'

'That may well be, Uncle, but I have to return to the academy, and the sooner the better.'

Unbidden, the thought of Forten came to the young Russell's mind and the unfinished business of the duel. His mother bent over and kissed him on the cheek.

'Oh Russell, must you go back? I was so looking forward to having you at home. I fret when you are away. I worry that you don't look after yourself. And by the pale look of you, you need looking after. Good food and a mother's love will do you the world of good.'

'A mother's love ... aye ... what about a wife's love. . . ?'

At that moment someone called out for a toast. The Danes turned towards their guests either missing or ignoring Russell's last remark.

'A toast to the Dane family. May they be happy and prosperous and live on here as our excellent and hospitable neighbours.'

There were cheers and much banter as the guests toasted the couple.

'Come friends, our cook has been preparing a feast,' Clive Dane announced. 'The tables have been set up outside. So everyone make your way out to the yard.'

The hum of conversation from the crowd grew in volume as they began to drift towards the back of the house. Russell was momentarily forgotten as his mother and uncle ushered the guests along. He leaned back against the wall. His thoughts were dark and he could not quell the dull ache of grief and unease that rose within him. His mother returned and took his arm.

'Come Russell,' she said, as she pulled him towards the doorway. 'I'm not going to cease nagging you till you promise to stay here with us. I don't want you going back to that horrible academy. I never wanted you to go in the first place. But I could not go against your father's wishes.

24

He thought it would do you some good. I think it has made you sad.'

'I am sad, Mother, but I shall stay here as you desire.'

And for a brief moment he felt a stir of guilt as again, unbidden, the unfinished duel surfaced in his mind.

6

The shots rang out suddenly, startling horses tied to the hitching rails. A young cowboy came stumbling out of the Cosmopolitan Saloon, a gun in his hand. He weaved about for a moment then staggered out into the middle of the street.

'Goddamn gonna tree this goddamn town.'

He raised the gun and loosed off a few shots into the air. He began to laugh drunkenly.

'I'm a rootin', tootin' son of a bitch from Hades. I'll outshoot and outdraw any galoot that dares to show his goddamn head out in the street.'

'Mathew,' a voice yelled out from inside the saloon. 'Where the hell are you?'

'Bernard, out here, you goddamn sonofabitch – out in the street.'

Again the saloon doors crashed open and another youth staggered onto the boardwalk. He was supporting his brother on one arm and in his other hand he held a whiskey bottle.

'We ain't finished drinking yet. You welshing out, you goddamn stomach-belcher? We still got this here bottle to finish.'

The youth addressed as Mathew hiccupped noisily. Wavering about, he pointed the pistol and shot in the direction of his brother. The bottle disintegrated as the bullet shattered the glass. Drunkenly, Bernard raised the hand that had held the bottle and stared blearily at the remnants of the neck still in his hand. Maurice hooted wildly.

'Goddamn you, Mathew, that bottle were three parts full. Why'd you go and do a fool thing like that for? I've a good mind to kick your goddamn ass for you.'

'Hell Bernard, can't you take a little joke? You're lucky I shot the bottle and not your goddamn hand off.'

The brothers staggered towards each other and met in the road. They threw their arms around each other and began to carouse drunkenly.

As I walked out in the streets of Elsinburg,
As I walked out in Elsinburg one day,
I spied a young cowboy all dressed in white linen,
All dressed in white linen and clothed for the grave.

Bawling out the next verses, the trio staggered down the middle of road. The citizens of Elsinburg wisely ignored the inebriated ruckus going on in their main street.

Still singing lustily, the brothers reached the livery stables and went inside. With much drunken banter they readied their mounts.

During these preparations Francis collapsed to the floor of the livery stable and began to snore.

'Hell, Francis ain't gonna make it back to the ranch in that state,' Bernard mumbled, staring down at his sleeping brother.

'Christ, Bernard, he ain't properly growed up yet. Hell, he's only just turned seventeen last birthday.'

He looked round the stable.

'Let's put him in a stall and leave him to sleep it off. You and I can cover for him back at the ranch. Hell, the new boss, Russell's uncle, won't know if he's short-handed or not.' He frowned suddenly. 'Can you believe he's marrying Russell's mother, Mrs Dane?' He shook his head in perplexity. 'He disappears for years somewhere down Texas and then, after all this time, comes home an' in next to no time he steps into his dead brother's shoes. Some men have all the luck. I wish I could meet a rich widder.'

He bent and grasped the younger brother under the armpits.

'Gimme a hand to drag Francis in here. He'll come to sometime tomorrow and ride out to the ranch.'

Their brother safely stowed, they mounted and rode out into the street and turned towards the ranch where they worked as cowhands for the Danes.

Their route took them past the cemetery. The youths urged their mounts faster as superstitious dread overcame them and they felt the need to hurry past the place of the dead. Inevitably, they glanced surreptitiously up at the prominent edifice of the Dane mausoleum.

'What the hell's that?'

The brothers hauled in their mounts and stared with some apprehension up the hill. The movement by the monument was fleeting but distinctive. A cloaked, hooded figure was seen momentarily as it ducked down by the edifice. The brothers stared with fixed eyes up at the monument. Sober, they might have made some sense of the apparition. Their senses befuddled with alcohol, they were filled with irrational terror.

'Ride, for God's sake, ride!'

They rammed spurs home and hastened away. Neither spoke till they had put some miles between themselves and the cemetery.

'Hell, Bernard, what was that?' Mathew's voice was unsteady as he spoke.

'Damnit, Mathew, I sure as hell don't know.'

'You don't think it were the devil? Sure looked like him all dark and cloaked like that.'

'Hell's bells, I sure don't know. It was at the Dane tomb, weren't it?'

'Sure was. What was the devil lurking round there for? Do you think it was come after Russell's pa? It sure scared the hell outta me.'

They rode in silence pondering on what they had seen.

'Maybe old man Dane was some sort of devil worshipper. You know he was sorta lucky in his life. He had a lovely wife. When that fella Forten challenged him he killed him in a duel and was acquitted of the crime of murder. After that he seemed to prosper. Everything he did turned to gold. His land increased in value. There was always good grass for the cattle. When he sold stock he allus got a good price.'

There was silence again as they measured these things against the man who had been their boss until his recent death.

'You think he sold his soul to the devil?'

'What do you think?'

'I dunno. It's possible. Why else is the devil hanging round the burial place?'

'You think Russell knows?'

The two cowboys shivered in the silence of the night.

'Only someone riding by there at night would know what was going on. Russell's been moping round the ranch this last while. Hardly talks to anyone. More than likely he don't know.'

Again they rode for a while pondering on the problem.

'One of us gotta tell him.'

'Hell, we tell him the devil's after his pa's soul?'

They rode on towards the ranch, surprisingly sober now after their fright.

'We're his friends. If we don't warn him who will?'

7

'Horace, by all that's holy, what brings you to Elsinburg?'

Russell greeted his old acquaintance with warmth that spoke of a long and deep friendship.

'I heard the news, Russell, of your father's death. I hurried here as soon as I could to see if I could be of any assistance.'

'Too late for the funeral but in time for my mother's wedding,' Russell enjoined, a hint of bitterness in his voice.

'Indeed, it did seem a mite hasty so soon after your father passed away.'

'Lets go into the Cosmopolitan. I'll buy you a drink. You must be thirsty after your journey. When did you arrive?'

'Last night, I ran into some of your pals, the Maxwell brothers.'

'Ah, were they sober?'

Horace laughed. 'They'd had a few. Come on, I'll take you up on that drink.'

The two friends stood at the bar and waited to be served. With two schooners of beer they drank each other's health.

'You miss your father, Russell?' Horace asked.

'He was like a solid shelter that fell asunder under the ravages of time, Horace. I do miss him. When he died, a part of me died with him.'

'Russell, I'm sorry to ask this, but how did your father die?'

'It was an accident. He fell in front of a runaway team and was dragged. By the time they found him he was dead. The horses' hoofs and the wagon wheels had pounded the life out of him.'

'I see. So it was sudden?'

'Yes, Horace, why do you ask?'

'Maybe it's the lawman in me.'

His friend pulled aside his coat revealing a marshal's badge. Russell gave a slow smile as he studied the other man.

'When I was drifting with no anchor, your pa took a fatherly interest in me to help me settle down. It was he as got me the job as lawman. As soon as I heard of your bereavement I asked for leave to come and see my old buddy.'

'You're not here in an official capacity, then?'

Horace thoughtfully eyed his friend for a moment before answering with a question of his own. 'You know much about your uncle?'

Russell frowned. 'I just know he went away after some scandal. There was a killing, but no one seems to know much about it. Beyond that I know nothing. Are you here to investigate his doings?'

The lawman shook his head.

'Russell, I'm not here on any business but to see you. I was just curious about your pa's death, that's all.'

'Horace, I know you better than that. Out with it. Something's troubling you.'

Horace took a long draught of beer before setting it carefully on the bar-top. 'Russell, how well do you know the Maxwell brothers?'

'Bernard, Francis and Mathew, why I know them as well as I know you. We grew up together. Why do you ask?'

'Russell, I'm not a superstitious fella, but they told me some strange tale. At first I was inclined to dismiss them as drunks but they were so earnest I began to wonder myself about what they had to tell.'

'Go on, you've whetted my interest.'

Horace took a deep breath, looked at his glass and then drained it. 'Lets have another.'

When the beers were refreshed the friends returned to their conversation.

'I'll give it to you straight. Riding home the other night, the Maxwells claim to have seen something hovering around the cemetery.'

Horace stopped and regarded his friend, awaiting his reaction. Russell stared into his drink. Around them the life of the bar carried on. The hum of conversation drifted up with the cigarette smoke. Men called to each other, joshed and laughed. The cackle of a woman's shrill laughter could be heard.

'If this is some sort of joke, Horace, I don't think it funny.'

'Russell, when the brothers told me their tale I reacted as you did. But they seemed so earnest. They begged me to talk to you about it.'

For a few moments Russell studied the man opposite

31

him. 'What does it mean, something hovering around the cemetery?'

'They claim on two occasions, late at night as they ride home from town, they see a thing in the cemetery – a dark shadowy shape. On these occasions the thing they claim to see is in the vicinity of your family tomb.'

'A thing in the cemetery! Horace, if this tale is designed to scare me or worry me it is succeeding. I will talk with the Maxwells. But if they are pulling a joke on me, it is in very bad taste.'

'I agree, Russell, but let us both talk with them. They promised to come into town this evening. If we all meet up here they can tell you their tale and you can decide what to do about it.'

Under protest, the Maxwell brothers had agreed to walk the short distance from the town to the cemetery. With the cowboy's inherent dislike of going anywhere without his horse, they complained unceasingly as they climbed the hill to the graveyard. Russell had intended placing his friends in various hiding places around the cemetery, but they had protested strongly.

'I ain't staying on my lonesome. We're keeping in a bunch. I wish now I hadn't told you about this here business,' grumbled Mathew.

'Such a bunch of gutless wonders I never came across in my life,' Russell said disgustedly. 'OK.' He pointed to low-growing bushes some way from the objective of their watch. 'Get in there, and stay awake. Horace and myself will be down the hill a bit.'

The watchers settled down in their allotted positions. Unbeknownst to Russell the brothers had thought to bring hip flasks. As soon as they were settled they began to indulge. The air of menace about their macabre surroundings tended to depress their natural high spirits.

'Hell, I'm scared,' admitted Bernard, shivering as he glanced around at the shadows.

Every dark shape and tombstone seemed to swell with sinister meaning. The brothers huddled closer together. The level in the flasks of bourbon sank significantly.

'Goddamn it, if something happens it'll sure scare the hell out of me,' observed Mathew. 'But if nothing happens I don't dare think what Russell will think of us.'

'Hush,' Mathew hissed. 'What the hell was that?'

8

'I hope those fellas keep awake,' grunted Russell.

The friends, having found a tombstone that had fallen over, used the levelled monument as a resting place.

'I wonder whose grave is this?' Horace remarked.

The lawman seemed unperturbed by their ghoulish vigil.

'Hell I know,' answered Russell. 'It's too dark to see anything. You got anyone buried here?'

'Nah, they all down Denver somewhere. Ain't been back there in a coon's age. Ma an' Pa died when I was young. It were your pa as took me in hand when he was senator. Bad business that killing he got mixed up with.' The lawman paused before continuing. 'Heard you had the same kinda bother with Forten the younger.'

'Yeah,' Russell replied, not pleased to be reminded. 'You heard about that. Unfinished business. . . ! What are folk saying about that?'

'Well, the ones as don't know you say you ran. I had to straighten them out about that. No Dane ever showed a yeller streak. Least not as far as I know.'

'There's always the first one, Horace.'

'Damnit, Russell, you know that ain't so.'

They both fell silent and peered up the hill towards the Dane sepulchre looming dark and menacing against the night sky.

At first Russell thought his eyes were playing tricks as he stared into the gloom. Something moved in the darkness about the tomb. An irrational and wild hope filled him. For one awful moment he thought his father had come to life and had managed to extricate himself from the tomb.

'Father,' he whispered.

'What?' hissed his companion.

But Russell did not answer. He was trying to focus on the movement at the tomb. At first it was vague and shadowy but then, as his vision sharpened, he saw a cloaked and hooded figure glide to the monument. Then all movement ceased and Russell began to think he had imagined the whole thing.

'There's someone or something up there,' Horace muttered. 'Goddamn it, Russell, are my eyes playing tricks on me?'

'Hell, I see it also.'

But the disturbance had stopped and both men peered anxiously up the hill, now unable to detect any movement. The low moan when it came unnerved them both.

'What the hell. . . !'

'I'm going up there.'

Russell stood up.

'I'll go with you.'

'No, you stay here,' Russell instructed. 'Whatever it is

34

might slip past.' He cocked his head to one side and listened. 'Nothing from them goddamn cowboys. I wonder if they saw anything.'

'Probably fast asleep by now.'

Russell began to clamber up the hill towards the family mausoleum. There was furtive movement by the tomb and a figure suddenly detached itself from the monument and began to move rapidly away.

'Halt, you up there. I want to talk to you.'

The shadowy figure kept moving. Russell began running, dodging tombstones as he went. He barked his shin and cursed. Limping slightly, he kept steadily following the moving shadowy figure.

'Russell!' one of the Maxwell brothers called. The voice sounded unsteady. 'What's going on?'

It was Horace who answered. 'Over here! Further up the hill!'

Russell knew he was gaining on his quarry.

'Stop!' he yelled. 'Be you friend or foe, I need to talk to you.'

He had no idea who or what he was chasing but he was not giving up. By now the mysterious figure had reached the outer fence. Russell tried to increase his speed as he saw the object of his pursuit working at the fence rails to make a way through. As the fence gave way, Russell flung himself at the dark figure. He cannoned into something soft and they both went down. By now he was fairly confident he was dealing with something of flesh and blood. The person screamed and struggled wildly.

'Gotcha!' Russell panted, as he landed on top and sat astride his capture. 'Now let's see who you are and what you're doing here at night.'

In the struggle the hood had come adrift and a mass of

hair tumbled out. Russell gasped and relaxed his grip.

'It's a female!'

A fist came from nowhere and hit him on the nose.

'Ouch!' he yelled in surprise and pain.

The woman gave a heave and Russell tumbled to one side. Then she was scrambling on all fours to get away from him.

'Damnit,' he muttered, as he recovered and launched himself after the crawling woman. This time when he got astride her he pinioned her arms. 'I ain't gonna hurt you. I just wanna know what the hell you were doing round my father's grave.'

All this while the woman was wriggling and struggling against him. Suddenly she ceased.

'Your father! Russell . . . let me up. I won't fight you no more.'

Slowly he stood and offered a hand to help her up.

'Who are you?'

For a brief moment she turned her face to him.

'Marian Lynas. Please let me go. I'll meet you later and explain what I was doing. Please.'

There were shouts from below as his companions searched for him. Slowly he nodded.

'All right then. Where?'

'Tomorrow night here. Come alone and I will tell you all.'

Then she was gone, leaving a bewildered young man behind her.

'Marian Lynas, what the hell was she up to here in the cemetery?' Russell muttered. 'Goddamn it, what the hell's going on?'

'Russell, where in tarnation are you?'

'Here,' called Russell.

He turned and re-entered the cemetery. After futile efforts to put the fence back again, he gave up and began walking down to meet his friends. They crowded round, plying him with questions.

'I dunno,' he lied. 'Whoever it was escaped through the fence. I was too late to stop them. Let's go back to town. This chasing ghosts has given me a thirst.'

By way of answer, Mathew Maxwell handed Russell a flask.

'Here, suck on that.'

A small dribble of liquor drained into Russell's mouth. 'Damnation, Mathew,' Russell said in disgust. 'What's the use giving me an empty bottle? You been sitting down there drinking all night instead of being on watch. No wonder the ghost got away.'

'Was it a ghost, Russell?'

'How the hell'd I know!' answered Russell. 'If you fellas had been more alert we may have caught it.'

They continued down towards the town debating the nature of the creature they had disturbed.

All the time Russell churned over in his mind the mystery of what the wife of the sheriff was doing in a cemetery late at night. And more especially, what interest did she have in the tomb of his father?

9

Marian Lynas was an attractive woman in her early thirties. Her brown hair was kept in a full and fluffy halo around her head. She had a lovely, wrinkle-free face with high cheekbones and a wide generous mouth. She was leaning against the Dane mausoleum, draped in the by now familiar cloak, when Russell stumbled up the hill to the grave. Gracefully she held out her hand for Russell to take.

'Can we be friends?' she asked.

Russell took her hand and, bending over it, kissed her gloved hand.

'I sincerely hope so.'

'Did you tell anyone about me and what happened last night?'

'No, ma'am.'

She moved further along the side of the tomb and traced a hand along the stonework. Russell obediently followed and waited patiently for whatever was to follow. As he covertly watched her she looked so feminine he suddenly felt contrite for the way he had manhandled her the previous night.

Finally she turned and faced him. He noticed her eyes in the moonlight were large and dark. Briefly he wondered what colour they were.

'I must apologise for chasing you the other night,' he began, but she shook her head, silencing him.

'Do not blame yourself. It was only natural for you to run me down. After all, you could have had no idea who I was or what I was up to. How come you were in the cemetery at that time of night?'

'Some friends of mine claimed to have seen a ghost lingering round my father's tomb. I felt obliged to investigate. I could ask you the same question. Why were you up here?'

She looked squarely at him as she replied. 'Your father and I were very good friends. I . . . I was greatly saddened by his death. No one knew of our friendship. My grief had to be private. That is why I came here – to weep for a wonderful man so foully done to death.'

Russell frowned.

'Friends, in what way friends?'

She looked down at her hands.

'What I tell you now must be in strictest secret. I must ask you to swear on the grave of your dear father not to reveal to a soul what I am about to tell you.'

'Tell me what?'

'First I must have your promise. I have asked you to swear on you father's grave.'

She waited patiently.

'Literally – to swear here and now?'

'You must if I am to tell you everything. Swear or I will go from this place and utter not another word.'

Tentatively he reached out his hand and laid it on the wall of the tomb.

'I swear on this, the grave of my father, that I will not reveal the things this woman will tell me tonight. On my father's soul I swear.'

He heard her sigh – a deep and forlorn sound in the night.

'When I say your father and I were friends I mean much more than friends.' She paused. 'Charles and I were lovers.'

Russell gaped. Lovers – it hardly seemed possible. Somehow he imagined his father and mother as pure in word and deed. Now he was told his father had been having an affair with another man's wife.

'But – your husband, Paul, did he know?'

Russell never had much to do with the sheriff of Elsinburg, much less his wife. The dour Paul Lynas was a severe looking man, much older than his wife. But then

Charlie Dane was older also. He shook his head, not understanding anything of this business.

'I always believed he knew nothing of Charles and myself. Now I am not so sure.'

Russell was silent, trying to make sense of this information she was imparting to him.

'I . . . I can see how you had to mourn in private. My friends believed you were a spirit of some sort. I had to come here and see for myself. I had the foolish notion something was disturbing my father's rest.' He smiled grimly. 'You certainly disturbed me and my friends.'

'I have some more disturbing news. You must tell no one of this conversation. Remember your oath.'

'Don't worry. I have no intention of revealing something so private. My father is dead. We must let his good name rest with him.'

'That is just the point. Do murder victims rest easy in their graves?'

'What? What are you saying – murder?'

She turned away from him and stared down – seeing the lights of the town through eyes that were brimming over with tears. He grabbed her arm and turned her to him.

'What are you telling me?' His voice was low and tense.

'Oh, dear God, that I did not have this to tell to the son of the man I loved most dear. Your father was murdered. Quite by accident I discovered it. I have lived and grieved with this knowledge. It has burned deep wells of sorrow into my soul.'

'Who? Who did this foul deed? Who was the murderer?'

'I believe it was my husband and one other.'

'Sheriff Paul Lynas murdered my father! But that is not possible. He's a law officer.'

'Do you think I do not know that! I tear myself apart

40

thinking I was the cause of his death from the jealousy of my husband.'

'You say your husband and one other – have you the name of that other fiend?'

'Yes, quite by accident I overheard him plotting the cover-up with Paul.'

His grip tightened. He did not realize he was hurting her till she gasped in pain.

'Tell me,' he urged, not relinquishing his grip.

Their faces were inches apart as he stared into her distraught face.

'Your uncle,' she whispered. 'Clive Dane, with my husband's help, murdered your father.'

He gave an anguished cry and turned from her. Then he was running blindly down the hill, heedless of obstacles in his path. Twice he tripped and fell but was up and running again, ignoring the bruising he endured from the unforgiving headstones. Blindly he fled from the terrible truth that had been revealed to him.

He did not hear the woman calling out to him.

She watched him running and when she could see him no longer she collapsed against the stone sarcophagus and began to sob. It was the terrible sound of a woman giving in to utter despair.

10

Marian Lynas closed the door gently behind her, then leaned against it. Her mind was in turmoil as she thought over the events of the last few nights.

Bitterly she regretted her confession to Russell Dane. The terrible secret had been festering inside her since the *accident* that had ended Charles Dane's life. She had not intended to go so far. Then again, Russell had a right to know about her relationship with his father. She had thought the telling of it to Russell would ease her own burden of guilt that she felt about the killing of her lover. Her mention of the murder had slipped out without her fully intending it.

Now she dreaded the consequences of her accusations. The secret of the murder was like a genie. Once out of the bottle there was no knowing what harm it would wreak. Unlike the genie, there was no way of putting it back. A cold sweat broke out on her as she recalled the youth's wild cry and his mad dash from the cemetery.

'Oh my God, what have I done?'

A match flared in the darkness of the room startling her. She stared with consternation as a lamp was lit. Sheriff Paul Lynas blew on the match and tossed the spent wood into a saucer. He turned up the flame and light flooded the room.

'Good evening, Marian. Up to your old tricks again?'

She said nothing, staring with ghastly fascination at her husband.

'You thought I did not know about Dane and you. I knew there was someone, but it took a long time to find out who.'

'Dane, I . . . I . . . what do you mean?'

'Why, Marian? Was it his power and position that attracted you? Perhaps his wealth?'

He took a thin cheroot from the table and, leaning over the lamp, sucked it into life.

'I suppose a lowly sheriff could not compete with a

senator and rich rancher. I always provided for you, Marian. We have a nice home here and a respectable place in society. Somehow it was not enough, though. Did he promise to divorce his wife and take you out to live in that grand house of his? Was that it, Marian? You and I know he would never have done that. There would be too much scandal attached to such a move. Dane hoped to run for senator again someday. A divorce would have ruined his chances. You were flogging a dead horse, Marian.' Suddenly he sniggered. 'Or should I say a dead senator?'

Her breathing was coming fast now. She clenched her hands and felt herself trembling all over.

'Please, Paul, this is all so unnecessary. You are making wild assumptions without a shadow of proof. What was Charles Dane to me? I knew him from when I was a little girl just as I knew you. He was purely an acquaintance.'

'What were you doing up at the cemetery?' he suddenly asked.

'What . . . the cemetery. . . ? I . . . I sometimes walk there at night. It is so peaceful and quiet. Why . . . why do you ask?'

'Last summer I hired a private detective,' he said changing tack. 'Cost me quite a packet as I had to have someone from out of the county. Couldn't have anybody as knows us poking round in our affairs or, more accurately, your affairs.'

'Detective. . . !' she mumbled indistinctly. The numbness and cold feeling of dread was growing steadily within her.

'Yeah.'

The lawman drew deeply on his cheroot and allowed the smoke to trickle from his nostrils.

'You see, I was kinda curious why you went off on your

own on buggy rides – sometimes late at night. Then there were those frequent visits to your sister over in Friedland. Happened to bump into her one day while I was over there on business. Wanted to know when you and I was gonna visit as she hadn't seen us in a while. Kinda surprised me as you had just been over there a day or so ago. Guess I musta been mistaken.'

She was frozen against the door, unable to move, as he sat in the room putting the case for the prosecution.

'You . . . you spied on me. . . ?' she managed feebly.

'Sure, when I asked you where you'd been you told me all sorts of stuff. I got kinda suspicious. A man don't live with a woman for ten years without getting a feel for these things.'

He reached behind him and she heard the clink of glass on glass as he poured a drink. It was only then she realized he had been drinking. The courage to confront her had come from a bottle of bourbon. A wave of contempt swept over her.

'What a despicable thing, spying on your own wife!'

He took a long swig from his glass before replying.

'Not so despicable as two-timing your husband.' His mood turned ugly. 'You found yourself another poor fool to play your game? Who were you meeting up at the cemetery?'

She moved away from the door.

'I'm going to bed. I'm tired of playing your little games.'

Suddenly he was out of his chair. She felt his arm come up and she was slammed violently against door.

'And I'm tired of your little games also,' he snarled, his face pushed up against her. 'Now you tell me who was up there at the cemetery tonight or do I have to beat it outta you!'

She was shocked. In all their married life Paul had never lifted a hand to her. The smell of alcohol was strong on his breath as he pinned her to the door.

'Stop it, Paul, you're drunk.'

He punched her in the stomach. The shock was such her legs went from under her and she slid to the floor. She was gasping with fright and pain. Then she started to weep.

'Tell me, you whore!'

His knee hit her in the chest. Her head banged against the door.

'Who was with you at the cemetery.'

'Russell Dane. . . !'

The confession was jerked from her, as she cringed before this uncharacteristic bout of violence.

Sheriff Paul Lynas stared down at the weeping women.

'Russell, surely he's a bit young even for you? What did you see him about?'

She made no reply. The sheriff slowly began the process of removing his belt.

'I guess I'll just have to beat it outta you.'

11

'Paul, how lovely to see you.' After greeting him, Gertrude Dane looked reprovingly at the sheriff. 'And where, may I ask, is Marian? Don't tell me you have come out to see us and not brought your wife?'

Sheriff Paul Lynas stood diffidently on the Dane porch with hat in hand and nodded regretfully.

'Howdy Gertrude, I'm afraid Marian isn't feeling too well today. She just wasn't up to the trip.'

'Oh dear, nothing too serious I hope. Maybe I should ride in and visit her.'

'No, no,' Sheriff Lynas said hastily. 'It's nothing serious. No need to bother yourself. I'm sure she'll be up and about in a few days. She suffers from these headaches from time to time. Just likes to shut herself up in a dark room and wait for them to go away.'

'The poor girl. Well, don't you forget to give her my love. Clive's in the drawing room. If you want to go through I'll get some coffee for you.'

Sheriff Lynas knocked on the door of the drawing room, pushed the door open and stuck his head inside. The new master of the Dane ranch was seated at a table surrounded by a mass of documents.

'Sheriff Lynas, come in, come in.' Dane threw his hands in the air in a gesture of irritation. 'You know, Paul, I can't make head or tail of these goddamn bills and statements. Gertrude reckons I oughta get to grips with it. Never was one for paperwork.'

He got up from the desk and walked to the fireplace.

'Here, join me in a cigar.'

They lit up and through the smoke Dane regarded his companion.

'What brings you out to the ranch, Paul? Are you here on business or social?'

'Russell knows.'

Clive Dane went very still. Slowly he walked to the large window and stared outside.

'What the goddamn hell you talking about, Lynas?'

'Marian told him. She overheard us discussing the cover-up. How we run a wagon over the body to make it look like

46

an accident. She went an' blurted it out to the kid.'

'Jesus H Christ, Lynas, you know what's at stake here? I'm about to take over the biggest and wealthiest ranch in the territory. Once I marry Gertrude I have everything. And now you tell me your goddamn wife is blabbing about our little secret.'

'Jeez, Dane, you think I don't know what's at stake! My job – my reputation – everything I've built up over the years. There's no way I wanna risk all that.'

'Who else she told?'

Lynas shrugged. 'As far as I can tell, no one else.'

'Can't you control your wife, Lynas? Goddamn it, are you master in your own house?'

'Yes, I do control her.' The lawman's voice was tight with fury as he spoke. 'She's locked in her room with a hiding she won't forget in a hurry. It's your nephew you gotta control.'

The door rattled and both men jerked their heads towards the sound. Gertrude Dane came bustling in carrying a tray.

'Coffee,' she announced brightly.

By the time she had settled the tray and began pouring, both men had control of themselves.

'Paul, have you seen any sign of Russell?' Gertrude asked as she handed the coffee to the sheriff.

'Why, no, ain't he at home?'

'Oh Paul, I do worry about Russell. He's been so moody lately. If you see him around town tell him to come on home. Tell him his mother wants to see him.'

'Sure, Gertrude. But I wouldn't worry about Russell. All boys go through the moody stage – or so I'm told.'

'I fear he's fretting over the death of his father,' Gertrude observed. She handed a cup to Clive Dane. 'I'll leave you to it.' She rose up on her toes and kissed him lightly on the cheek.

'Are you staying for lunch, Paul?'

'No thanks, ma'am. I've a busy day ahead of me.'

As soon as Gertrude was gone, Dane looked speculatively at the sheriff. 'Tell me exactly what went on between Russell and your wife.'

'From what I can make out she was visiting the grave at night, mooning over your goddamn dead brother, when the kid grabbed her. Whatever the cause, she shot her mouth off about you and me fixing to kill Charlie Dane. She says the kid ran off blubbering his eyes out. No one's seen him since.'

'We gotta fix Russell and that wife of yours. Him on his own mouthing off about us shouldn't cause too many waves, but if Marian backs him up we're in trouble. Lynas, you gotta shut that kid's mouth for good.'

'Hell, Clive, why me? I'm supposed to be the law. You can kill him just as readily as me.'

'Damn you for a lily-livered excuse of a man! No wonder your wife went off with my brother. You know I can't touch the kid. If even a hint of this gets out I'll be finished with Gertrude. I gotta marry her. After that I don't give two hoots what Gertrude or, for that matter, what other people think. Once I got power of attorney I can start selling stuff and get my hands on some real dough. Now you do your part and silence that kid.'

Sheriff Lynas was white-faced as he confronted his partner in crime. His hand strayed to his holstered Colt as he stared with real hatred at Clive Dane. 'Nobody talks to me like that,' he gritted out, 'nobody.'

Dane leaned towards the lawman. There was a cold glint in his eyes. Lynas was the first to shift his gaze.

'How do you suggest I do it?' the lawman asked sullenly.

Dane turned and walked to the window.

'You say you beat up on Marian.'

'Yeah,' the lawman answered uneasily. 'Why.'

'Why don't you send a message to the kid pretending it's from Marian asking him to meet her at home? When he arrives, you kill him. The story you tell is, you came home unexpectedly and found Russell attacking Marian. You shot him before you knew who it was. Marian has the bruises to prove your case. And this time make sure she keeps her goddamn mouth shut.'

12

'Marian.'

She stared fearfully at her husband standing framed in the doorway. After he had beaten her he had locked her in her room. She was hurt, tired, hungry and scared.

'I'm sorry I hit you, Marian. I was out of my mind with drink and . . . and jealousy. I know that's no excuse. Come downstairs. I made something to eat.'

She sat at the dining-room table while he served her up a bowl of steaming soup and a plate of biscuits.

'Marian, can we start again. Put all this Dane business behind us. I . . . I know you think I had a hand in the death of Charlie Dane. I . . . it wasn't like you think. All I did was cover up for Clive. He wanted his brother out of the way. I swear to God I never wanted him dead but I thought at the time it would scare him away from you.'

She kept her head bowed as she sipped the soup. Hungry as she was, now that the food was before her she did not feel like eating. Nevertheless she went through the

49

motions of spooning the soup and nibbling at a biscuit.

'Now I want to make amends. Please believe me Marian. I want to make it up to young Russell Dane – to tell him the truth of what happened that night.'

At last she looked across the table at him.

'The truth?'

His face looked wrinkled and haggard. His hair was receding back along his skull. When her parents died leaving her alone, he had been most kind to the insecure young orphan. He had arranged the funeral – saw to her being lodged in a decent house. As time passed he had been a frequent visitor till the day he had asked her to marry him. And she had accepted – because he was dependable, kind, considerate, respectable, secure.

There was no love in the marriage arrangement. For her it was security – for him it was the acquisition of a charming young girl for his wife. All that had changed when Charlie Dane had cast his eye upon her.

There had been some truth in the cruel jibes her husband had thrown in her face the other night. In her heart she had wanted to take the place of Gertrude Dane and become the mistress of the Dane ranch.

'Aye, Marian. He has to know the truth about his uncle. I believe the boy might be in some danger.'

She frowned at that, then her eyes widened. 'You don't think. . . ?' She left the unthinkable unspoken.

'Clive Dane is a ruthless and dangerous man. I made some enquiries about him after he suddenly reappeared following his long absence. It seems he has a certain reputation down in Texas. As far as I could find out, he was a hired gun.'

'A hired gun, what does that mean?'

'It means just that – he was a paid killer. Hired his gun

out for money. Please believe me, Marian, I had no hand in Charles Dane's death. God forgive me, I just covered up for Clive.'

She was unsure – wanted to believe him. Since the death of Charles Dane her world had crumbled around her: the golden dreams of a future with the richest man in the county – the lady of the manor; then the thrashing she had received at the hands of her husband. She had never experienced violence in her life. Suddenly, in a very short time, her lover was killed and she herself was subjected to the attacks of a jealous husband. She was scared – anxious – wanting everything to return to normal.

'We need to warn young Dane. I could never live with myself if something happened to that kid. In a way it would make up for my failure in preventing the death of his father.'

'What are you going to do?'

'It will be best if it came from you. He'll be suspicious of me, seeing as you told him I was involved in the death of his father.'

'How . . .' She indicated her bruised face. 'I don't want to be seen out like this.'

'Write him a note. Tell him to come here. I'll go down to the office and stay there. I can stay all night if needs be. Just warn him about his uncle. If he suspects his nephew knows about the killing of his brother then that kid is in real danger.'

'Can't you protect him? Arrest Clive Dane?'

'And what would that achieve?' She detected a hint of bitterness in his voice. 'Dane would squeal like a pig – implicate me in the killing. No, we warn the kid. At least that way he can be on his guard. But tell him . . . tell him I had no hand in his father's killing. I admit I was involved in the cover-up but I regret that now.'

So she wrote the note as he dictated it to her. As sheriff of the town it was easy for him to move around and he planted the note in the whore's room and just hoped she would deliver it.

Then he went down to his office from where he could get a good view of the Cosmopolitan. While he waited, he cleaned his pistol. When that was done he eyed up the long guns in his gun rack, then decided his pistol was enough. Bringing home a rifle would smack too much of a man expecting trouble.

He was an accomplished pistol man. Not that he would be in the same league as Clive Dane. A man did not gain a reputation as a hired gun without being proficient with a sidearm. Dane would be fast and dangerous. He was also vicious.

Sheriff Lynas had every reason to know how vicious. The night they killed Charlie proved that. Clive had battered his brother unconscious while the sheriff had held him. To cover up the crime they had rolled the wagon over the injured man. Clive was not satisfied till he was certain his brother was dead. They had left the body to be found.

It was the sheriff's painful duty to ride out to the ranch and inform his widow of the death of her husband. It was plainly an accident. There was no need for an inquest. Charlie Dane was buried and that should have been the end of the affair. No one suspected anything. Clive was well placed to woo the grieving widow. And Sheriff Paul Lynas was rid of the man who had cuckolded him.

Now the son of the murdered man, his suspicions roused, was poking into the affair. It was as if the ghost of Charlie Dane had risen from the grave to point the finger of accusation at his killers. Tonight that ghost would be laid to rest. Russell Dane would join his father in the family mausoleum.

13

'Draw – aim – fire.'

The shots rang out – close spaced.

'No, no, no, no, no. Aim. You're just pulling the gun and firing. Take your time. Aim at what you're firing at. Imagine pointing your finger. Take the time to point and then squeeze the trigger.' Horace shook his head in mock despair. 'The impatience of youth. Russell, won't you tell me why you want to learn how to draw a fast gun?'

Russell slowly holstered the heavy Colt.

'I wanna be like Billy the Kid and kill twenty-one men before my twenty-first birthday.'

'Russell, you know that's hogwash. Now tell me the truth or I'll quit this instructor's job.'

'Hell, Horace, it's no big deal. I just wanna protect myself. Look what happened to Pa. Forten called him out and he had to defend himself At the academy the same thing happened to me. I got enemies. If I don't stand up to them one of them's gonna gun me down.'

'I don't know, Russell. I feel there's something you ain't telling me.'

The two friends eyed each other for a few moments. At last Horace shook his head.

'All right, once more. Draw – aim – fire. Remember that sequence. There's no good being fast if you can't hit what you're aiming at.'

The lessons continued.

'That's good, that's a vast difference. When you've mastered that sequence then you can practice speed. But never sacrifice accuracy for speed. A steady nerve means a steady hand.'

Russell's wrist was aching when, because of failing light, the friends decided to call a halt to the lessons in gun craft. The continual pulling and firing the heavy weapon was taking its toll. But Russell was quite pleased with his efforts.

'Let's go back to town and have a drink, Horace. That's one technique I'm certainly getting good at.'

'Yeah, you certainly earned a drink. You've made good progress this afternoon.'

By the time they got back to the Cosmopolitan, the saloon was crowded. There was no sign of the Maxwell brothers as the two friends elbowed their way to the bar. Nursing a bottle of whiskey, they fought their way to the stairs and sat on the steps where they supped and discussed their future plans.

'Russell, I gotta get back to my patch again. As I told you, I came here to pay my respects to your pa. Now I must return to my duties.'

'Horace, I'll be real sorry to see you go. When do you leave?'

'Tomorrow, I should have gone sooner but . . .' The lawman shrugged. 'You seemed so lost, I guess I overstayed.'

'You're a good friend, Horace.'

'Russell, no matter what happens you can call on me for help anytime. I owe your pa everything. I sure would welcome the chance to repay his good offices.'

Two good-looking young men soon attracted the attentions of the bargirls. They gathered round and began the ritual of drinking and seduction that was the tools of their trade.

'I got something for you, Russell,' crooned one large, busty girl with a round chubby face and a head of luxurious red hair.

54

'You know I'm partial to redheads.'

She giggled.

'I might want to check it out if you are a real redhead.'

The girl giggled some more as she fished around inside her full bosom, finally coming up with a crumpled envelope.

'I was told to give this to you.'

Russell frowned as he took the creased missive. 'Ah,' he quipped, 'to have been where this has been and come up all limp and wrinkled. . . .'

His name was printed on the envelope in an uneven and childish hand.

'Who gave you this?'

'It was left in my room.'

She did not tell him the letter had come with a five-dollar bill attached. Standing up and moving away from the stairs, Russell ripped open the envelope.

Tonight late at the house Paul away. Have important news.

Slowly he read the note again. Thoughtfully he folded the paper and shoved it in his pocket. In view of the events of the last few days he had no doubt whom the note was from.

'Come upstairs, Russell,' the redhead invited. She smiled seductively. 'I can guarantee I am a genuine redhead. With someone like you I could burst into flaming passion.'

He laughed but was not tempted. The face of Marian Lynas intervened.

Come late. I have important news.

Since her shocking revelation in the cemetery he'd had no peace. Tempting as it had been to block out the ghastly secret she had imparted to him with the assistance of girls and drink, he had imposed a limit on his indulgences. Never for a moment had he doubted her version of events.

The official story had been very different. A team of runaway horses had dragged Charlie Dane thus causing his death. An unfortunate accident. It was certainly a clever ruse. There were no witnesses. Cowhands had found the body badly mutilated. It was obvious what had happened.

To cement the case, the strong smell of whiskey had been present on the body. Some had even spilled onto the victim's shirt. It was an open and shut case. Sheriff Lynas was not looking any further into the accident.

Confronting the men involved in his father's killing would accomplish nothing. Ranged against the youngster were the sheriff of the town and the brother of the deceased. He could visualize the smooth confident face of his uncle smiling that sleek smile.

'Come now, Russell. The death of your father has unhinged you. Grief sometimes does that.'

Russell reasoned he would have to bide his time and chase his own way of dealing with the situation. If that meant learning to handle a gun, then that's what he was doing. When he was ready, he would bring his own brand of justice to his father's murderers.

But not just yet – not just yet. When he was ready!

14

The two friends came out onto the boardwalk and stood facing each other.

'Hell, Horace, do you need to leave tomorrow? At least wait another day.'

The burly lawman smiled ruefully his young friend. 'Gotta go, Russell. Duty calls. A lawman's life is not his own. The longer I stay away the more unruly my own patch becomes.' He put his hand out and they gripped hard.

'Look after yourself, Russell. I might see you at breakfast. The stage leaves first thing in the morning. In case I don't see you, just you keep practicing that draw. I just hope you never have to put it to the test.' He paused for a moment as he reflected on his friend's need to become handy with a sidearm. 'You know you made a quip today that you wanted to be like Billy the Kid and have a score of killings under your belt before your twenty-first birthday. Well, just remember how young the Kid was when Pat Garrett shot him down. Those who live by the gun perish by the gun. But remember, if you ever need me you just have to call and I'll come arunning.'

With that he turned and headed down to the boarding house to get a night's sleep before starting out on his journey in the morning.

Russell watched his friend go with some regret. Then he turned and looked about him. There was very little activity in the streets of Elsinburg at that time of the night. Most of the action was in the saloons and gambling halls. It would be the small hours of the morning before the drinkers and gamblers stumbled out into the streets to head for homes, wherever or whatever that might be. Slowly he began to walk.

Marian Lynas had summoned him to impart some more information. A nervous anticipation twitched at his guts. He tried to shrug away the feeling of unease. Nothing she could tell him would have the same unsettling devastation on his mind as her first revelation regarding the death of his father. He walked softly and cautiously, anxious not to be seen.

Once away from the main street with its saloons and places of entertainment, the night seemed lonely and quiet. He listened to his own footsteps and wondered if his father had walked down these streets for his secret assignations with Marian Lynas. His father's infidelity was almost as shocking to the young man as was the brutal truth of his murder.

'Senator Charlie Dane,' he said aloud. 'Unfaithful husband.'

Did his mother know her husband was unfaithful? He stopped beside a picket fence. The house behind him was silent. He was in the residential part of the town.

'Everything quiet as a grave.'

Suddenly he wanted a smoke. He had never been a smoker but here in the dark somehow the urge to stop and bide his time with the ritual of rolling a cigarette and striking a light suddenly took on a strange appeal.

'First thing tomorrow, I'll buy myself the makings.'

He could see the Lynas house from where he stood. There was a light on downstairs. Marian Lynas, the woman who had seduced his father sat waiting for him. The thought strangely excited him. He walked on, a nervous agitation building up in him.

Again he stopped, looking around to see if he was being observed. The road seemed deserted. Nearby a dog began barking. This set off other dogs in the vicinity. Russell peered hard into the gloom of the night, wondering what had disturbed the dog. He could see nothing to rouse his suspicions. Cautiously he moved on, wondering if he should go to the front of the house or round the back. In the end he went to the front door and knocked softly.

The tension built in him as he waited. At last the door opened and he saw a woman standing inside the hallway.

'Mrs Lynas?'

The light was too dim to make out her features. She stepped back and beckoned him inside, pausing to look

58

into the road before closing the door.

'Thanks for coming, Russell. Go on in.'

There was only one lamp lit in the living room and it was turned low.

'Do you want a drink or anything?' She sounded as nervous as he felt.

'No thanks, ma'am. Don't go to any trouble.'

'Have a seat.'

He sat in a chair and she sat opposite. Her hair hung loose around her face. This combined with the dim light prevented him from seeing her face properly.

'You said you had something important to tell me.'

He could see her hands pale in the low light moving nervously in her lap as she clasped and unclasped them.

'The things I said the other night were only partly true. I was mistaken about some of the facts.'

Somewhere in the house a floorboard creaked. Russell tensed. 'What was that?'

'What was what?'

'Are we alone here?'

'Yes, Paul is out on business. There's just you and me here. Why do you ask?'

'I thought I heard something at the back of the house.'

The flame in the lamp flickered wildly as a breeze wafted through from somewhere in the house. Unconsciously, Russell slid his hand on to the handle of the Colt he had been firing all afternoon. In the shadows of the room his movement was unseen.

'Oh, don't worry about that. In this old house there's always noises of some sort. I suppose I've become used to them.'

'What was it you got wrong, then?'

'I . . . I told you Paul was involved in the murder of your

father. That was only partially true. He . . . he did not do anything bad. What he did do was help cover up the deed. He felt justified because of what he believed was going on between your father and me. . . .'

'What are you saying? My uncle killed my father and your husband conspired to conceal the crime. Why would he do that if he weren't in on the murder? What hold has my uncle over the sheriff?'

'I . . . I don't know, only maybe he knew about Charlie and me and threatened to expose the affair. I . . . I don't know. I just know he regrets what he did and wants to make it up to you.'

Russell was silent for a moment as he thought over what she was telling him.

'That's what you wanted to tell me – that the sheriff regrets helping a murderer escape?'

'It was more than that. He wanted to warn you about your uncle. He fears that once he finds out you know about the murder then he might want to kill you too.'

The flame in the glass chimney fluttered wildly. Russell felt a draft on the back of his neck. Instinctively he rolled off the chair overturning it as he fell. Flame lanced out, lighting up the room in brilliant luminosity. At the same time the crash of a revolver blasted out.

15

Marian Lynas cried out once and then was quiet. Russell lay where he was curled up on the carpeted floor. As he went down he had pulled his Colt. Slowly he eased it forward, searching for a target. A shadowy figure moved into the room.

'Marian, sorry about this. I mistook him for someone else.'

The voice was that of Sheriff Lynas. He moved to the lamp and turned up the wick. Bright light flooded the room. Russell remained still, his Colt trained on the sheriff. His mind was in a whirl. Marian Lynas had set him up for her husband to bushwhack him. Anger began to surge in him like a black tide.

'Marian . . . dear God . . . Marian.'

Sheriff Lynas was bending over his wife. He shook her shoulder. Her head lolled to one side.

'Marian. . .! Dear God, what have I done?'

'Lynas, you treacherous, murdering bastard!'

Sheriff Lynas whirled to face the owner of the voice – his own countenance a white mask of shock. The gun was still in his hand. He fired instinctively and for a moment a puzzled look crossed his face as his shot blasted across the room and hit the wall. It did not occur to him to look down for the source of the voice.

Lying on the floor, Russell had his own gun aimed and ready. Almost without volition he triggered. He could not miss the tall figure towering over him. The sheriff staggered back under the impact of the bullets. He managed to let off one more shot from his own weapon before tumbling back into the table that held the lamp.

Everything went over with a crash. A shocked and shaken Russell lay where he was for a moment. At last he clambered to his feet. Around the inert body of the sheriff a pool of paraffin was gathering. A small blue flame ignited and began to spread.

Hastily, Russell stamped on the burgeoning flames. The

smell of cordite and singed clothing and spilt fuel filled the little room. Russell tried to put his gun away and discovered he was trembling violently. It was with great difficulty he inserted the barrel into the holster and rammed the weapon home.

'You set me up, Mrs Lynas. You lured me here for your murdering husband to kill me.'

Marian Lynas made no answer. Suddenly there were voices outside and someone hammered on the front door.

'Sheriff Lynas! Sheriff! What's going on?'

'Mrs Lynas, is anyone there?'

The voices were querulous and insistent from the front of the house.

'I heard shots. I'm sure they came from here.'

More hammering on the door. Russell looked at the body of the sheriff sprawled on the floor. With no light in the room it was hard to make out details. His wife had still made no move.

'Mrs Lynas . . . Marian. . . ?' As he spoke, Russell moved to the sitting figure and put out his hand.

'The goddamned door was unlocked all the time,' someone shouted.

'Hello the house. Anyone at home?'

Russell put out a trembling hand and touched Marian Lynas.

'Get a light,' someone yelled. 'It's dark as pitch in here.'

There was a wet sticky substance on the front of Marian Lynas's dress. Russell stared at the dark stain on his fingers. The door burst open. A lamp was held up to light the room.

'What the hell. . . !' a man swore.

'Dane . . . Russell Dane! What the hell's going on?'

'Good God, is that blood?'

'Dane, get the hell away from there.'

'It's Sheriff Lynas – on the floor . . . he's been shot!' another voice cut in.

Rough hands seized the youth.

'There's blood on his hands.'

'Damnit, the kid's killed the sheriff and his wife.'

'Wait,' Russell tried to protest.

A fist clubbed him to the ground.

'Get his gun.'

'Goddamn murderer!'

'Oh my God, this is terrible.'

Roughly they pulled Russell from the room. Hard hands were gripping him.

'Take him down the jail. We can hold him there till we decide what to do with him.'

'Find the jailhouse keys. Might be on the sheriff's body.'

'Listen, I'm trying to tell you what happened.'

Someone hit him in the mouth. He fell back, was pulled upright and punched and kicked outside.

'Found the keys,' a triumphant yell from the room.

'Let's take him down the jail.'

The outraged citizens of Elsinburg frogmarched their prisoner down the road. They unlocked the office where earlier that evening Sheriff Lynas had sat and waited for Russell to emerge from the Cosmopolitan. Now the sheriff lay dead along with his wife. The good citizens had caught the killer literally red-handed.

They had found him in the house with the blood of Marian Lynas on his hands. It was an open-and-shut case. No judge in the land would have a qualm about hanging the culprit.

Russell lay bruised and bleeding in his cell.

'Goddamn Marian Lynas and her goddamn murdering husband.'

Morning was a long time coming. Russell watched the light in his cell slowly grow as the sun lit up the outside world. All night he had wrestled sleeplessly with his confused thoughts.

How much of what Marian Lynas had told him was true? She was somehow tied up with the murder of his father. It was for certain Sheriff Lynas and his wife wanted him dead. They had lured him to their home in order to kill him – that much was obvious. The thing he wanted to know was the extent of his Uncle Clive's involvement in the murder plot.

His head ached. He wanted a drink. No one had come near him since he had been locked in last night.

'Hi. Anyone out there? I need a drink.'

There was no answer. He clambered up on his bunk to the barred window but all he could see was the side of a clapboard building.

'Damnit. I could die of thirst and starvation.'

There was the rattle of keys from the front of the building. He waited expectantly. Footsteps and voices echoed inside and the door separating cells from the main office opened. A couple of townspeople came inside. They stared curiously at the prisoner.

'It's OK, let her through.'

It was his mother. She came inside, pale-faced, distraught and with anxious eyes.

'Oh Russell, what is happening?'

She held her hands out towards him as she came forward. 'They say you killed Sheriff Lynas and Marian. Tell me it isn't true.'

'Ma, I swear to God I never killed Marian. Her husband killed her.'

There was a snort of derision from the man that had let

64

his mother through. 'I'll leave you alone, Mrs Dane. Just come on out when you're ready.'

'Russell, what's to be done? I'm at my wit's end to think of what might happen to you.'

'Where's Clive? I thought he would've come in with you.'

'He's back at the ranch. When he heard what happened he wanted to gather the hands and come in and break you out of jail. I persuaded him not to. I didn't want any more trouble piling up on your head. Clive wouldn't come in with me for he said he feared he might take the law into his own hands and do something foolish to get you free.'

'Yeah, I'm sure,' Russell retorted bitterly.

'Russell, what's to do?'

'First, go get Horace Winterman. He's staying at Mrs Hounslow's. Hurry before the stage leaves. Otherwise you'll miss him. Tell him what's happening.'

'The stage, we met it on the way in.'

Russell stared at his mother, a slow feeling of dread creeping over him. He had banked on Horace being here to help him. Now he was alone.

The way the townsmen had reacted to his version of events showed him how people would view his behaviour. He had a horrible feeling he had been found guilty before even an inquiry had got under way.

16

'I say hanging's not enough. Tar an' feather an' flog him, an' then hang him.'

There was a rumble of approval from the crowd gathered in the makeshift courtroom. The bar of the Cosmopolitan was the only place big enough to accommodate the crowd that wanted to attend the trial of Russell Dane for the brutal murder of Sheriff Lynas and his wife.

A table had been set up in front of the bar and three of the leading citizens of Elsinburg were seated behind this – chosen to preside over the trial. To one side, Russell sat on a chair facing the crowd with an armed deputy each side of him. With handcuffed hands resting on his lap he looked young and vulnerable. He never raised his head but stared down at the floor.

'Order, I say order there. No unhelpful remarks from the floor. Any more interruptions and this court will be held in camera.'

There were mutterings from the crowded saloon but no one interrupted, very few quite knew what 'in camera' meant and no one wanted to show their ignorance by asking. The proceedings got under way.

'We've assembled this court of law to try Russell Dane for the crime of murder. Certain witnesses will be called to testify as and when this duly elected court deems it fit to call the said witnesses to assert the facts.'

George Perivale was the owner of the large grocers and provisions store in the town, and he considered himself something of an expert on everything. It was he who led the court and held everyone in awe with his pedantic pronouncements.

'Talk in American, George,' someone in the crowd called.

'Silence in court,' George retorted and banged on the table top with a mallet he had brought from his shop for the task. 'This court is in session.'

'Call the first witness.'

One by one the witnesses were called. They had been the men first on the scene at the house where the murder had been committed. All told the same story in varying detail.

Shots had been heard in the home of Sheriff Paul Lynas and his wife Marian. When the witnesses finally entered the house, the sheriff and his wife lay dead. The accused had been found with blood on his hands and in his holster was a Colt .44. The gun had recently been fired. Sheriff Lynas's gun was on the floor where he had dropped it after being shot by the accused. The sheriff's gun had also been fired in an attempt to protect himself against his killer.

Other witnesses came forward and testified that Dane in the past days had been practicing with his gun under the tutelage of a mysterious gunman. At the end of the witness examinations George was moved to sum up the case for the prosecution.

'It appears to me this young man had a grudge against Sheriff Lynas. He was practicing with his gun with the objective of bracing the deceased, and in the shootout he killed the sheriff and his wife.

'Now, there may be some doubt that the accused intended to kill Mrs Lynas. It may have been a stray bullet hit her. In any case this young man was responsible for her death.' George Perivale turned his head and contemplated the youth slumped nearby. 'Has the accused anything to say before this court passes sentence?'

Sunk in self-pity, Russell was not taking much notice of the proceedings going on around him. One of the deputies nudged him and he looked up, unsure what was expected of him.

'I said, has the accused anything to say in his defence?'

Russell blinked uncertainly before speaking. 'I . . . I went to the house because Marian . . . Mrs Lynas had something to tell me.'

'How did you know she wanted to see you?'

'She sent me a note, telling me to come to her house.'

'Where is this note?'

Bemusedly, Russell began to pat at his clothes. His task was hindered somewhat by his cuffs. After some effort he produced a crumpled paper from a back pocket.

'I guess this is it.'

George read the note.

'Humph, anyone know Marian's handwriting?'

'Hell with all this nonsense! Let's take him out and hang him. Dirty, murdering scum!'

A low grumble of agreement came from the crowd.

'Let's do it now. All we need is a rope and a tree limb.'

George was hammering hard on the table with his mallet.

'Order, order! We do this good and proper.'

'A man what kills another man and his wife in their own home don't deserve good and proper. He deserves what he gave Paul and Marian.'

The griping voices grew louder.

Gertrude Dane stared with stricken eyes at the man she was to marry.

'They think my son is guilty of murder. Russell is no murderer. This whole thing is a terrible mistake.'

Clive Dane moved towards his brother's widow. He put out his arms to comfort her.

'Don't, Clive. Don't touch me. This whole thing has broken my heart. First I lose Charles and now I am to lose my son. It is too much for a woman to bear. I . . . I don't know what I'll do if anything happens to Russell. I . . . I'll sell up everything and go back east to live with my sister. I couldn't live here with so many awful memories.'

Gertrude did not see the flicker of alarm that passed across her brother-in-law's face at her sentiments.

'Gertrude, they won't do anything to Russell. They'll throw him in jail for a spell. We'll hire a good lawyer and a private detective if necessary.'

Hoof beats sounded outside in the yard. They both looked towards the sound. In a moment someone was hammering on the front door. They found Bernard Maxwell on the porch. He snatched off his hat when he saw Gertrude.

'Howdy, Mrs Dane, came as fast as I could. They're having a trial in town. The townsfolk are trying Russell for murder. I've left my brothers Francis and Mathew to keep an eye on things. Those folk – they're all riled up about Russell. Some are talking about lynching. I . . . I thought you oughta know. . . .'

Gertrude Dane put a hand to her throat and reeled against the side of the door. She gave a little mew of despair. Clive moved to her side and put a supporting arm around her shoulders. Her tragic eyes stared up at him.

'Russell – I'll have to go to him,' she whispered hoarsely. She turned from the two men and called over her shoulder. 'Bernard, hitch up my buggy. I'm riding into town immediately.'

For a moment Clive's lips tightened. The hint of something savage flickered in his eyes, then was shuttered down. 'Hold fire, Gertrude. This is a job for a firm hand. Let me handle this.' He turned to Bernard. 'Go get those two new hands I hired last week – the two Texans. Tell them to saddle up and bring their irons. Gertrude, you stay here at the ranch. I'll bring my nephew home should I have to tree the whole goddamn town.'

For a short moment Gertrude stared at her husband-to-be. Hope shone in her eyes. 'Clive, if anyone can do it I know you can. I will wait here for you.'

Suddenly, she flung her arms around the big man and hugged him hard. He smiled over her shoulder as he patted her.

'Don't you fret. We'll bring our boy home.'

He went inside the house and re-emerged a few moments later with a pistol strapped to his waist. At the same time, Bernard Maxwell rode up leading a saddled horse. Behind him came two cowhands. They were lean and tanned. They looked hard at Clive Dane.

'Boys, we got some hard riding to do and there may be some shooting at the end of it. We're riding into Elsinburg. You two back me up no matter what the play. They're fixing to lynch my nephew. I aim to stop them even if it means gunplay.' He swung up on the spare horse Bernard had brought. 'Marian, you get lunch ready. Young Russell'll be mighty hungry when we bring him back.'

17

'Order! Order! Order in court.'

'Order my foot. It's a hanging we want. Not order.'

'The kid's a killer. We wanna make sure he don't kill again.'

'His pa was a killer. Like father like son.'

There was no reasoning with them. They were a mob. Rough, drunken men surged around the bar overturning the judge's table. George the grocer scrambled from the wreckage and scurried out of danger. The deputies backed

70

away from the angry faces. They'd only been sworn in that morning to do guard duty at the trial.

'Hell, fellas, you can't take the law into your own hands,' one protested feebly.

'Terence, you just look the other way while we do just that.'

Russell tried to fight them. His cuffed fists caught one of them in the mouth drawing blood. Swearing loudly they piled on him, giving him no room to swing. Desperately he kneed a big, bearded cowboy in the groin. The man cursed and swung away. Another face took his place. Russell drove his head forward at a townsman in a suit. Someone punched the youngster from behind. As he went forward he swung his cuffed hands and caught a suited man in the ear.

There was cursing and frenzied activity as the crowd boiled around him, anxious to get at the victim. He was kicked and punched a dozen times. There were just too many. He went down and booted feet kicked him so that he had to curl into a ball in an effort to protect himself.

'Get him outside. There's a tree by the livery stable. I seen fellas hanged there afore.'

He fought them all the way. It was a hopeless cause.

'You don't know what you're doing. I'm innocent. Sheriff Lynas was involved in the murder of my father. He wanted to shut me up.'

If anyone heard or understood him they just ignored his protestations.

'Anyone got a rope?'

'We'll get one from the livery.'

The crowd spilled into the street pushing their captive roughly through the swing doors. A boot struck Russell in the back. He stumbled forward trying desperately to keep on his feet. The mob was growing more and more angry – their anger increased because some of them had been injured by the prisoner's fight back. They did not expect a mere kid to battle so ferociously.

They were not individuals anymore but a blood-crazed rabble. The mob was a hungry animal scenting blood. All notions of fairness and decency had fled. Unreasoning hatred and anger seethed within them. Primitive man was on a killing spree. Taken separately and isolated from the mob hysteria, each man could not have given a coherent reason for his anger.

Young Russell Dane was to die on a tree. The men involved would wake up next morning and make excuses for what had happened. All remorse would be buried or justified.

In the livery stable there was a delay while men disappeared inside in search of the means of execution.

'Over there – that goddamn tree. They hanged Pete Thompson there a few years back.'

'I remember that. He shot old man Coleman over a card game.'

Two men emerged triumphant from the livery brandishing a coiled rope. 'This oughta do the trick.'

'Make a noose. Gotta make a proper noose.'

'Here let me. I worked for the army. Have to do this right.'

A rough noose was fashioned and displayed to the excited crowd.

'Damn thing oughtta work. That's a proper hangman's noose.'

'Got the thirteen coils, has it?'

'That's just goddamn superstition.'

'Ain't so. Thirteen's for the thirteen colonies – thirteen

stripes on the flag. We hangin' him lawful and fittin' with a proper legal noose.'

'Hell, who cares! Lets get on with the hanging.'

'Get a horse! Gotta set him on a goddamn horse.'

Again, men ran inside the livery stable to find a horse on which to set the condemned man.

Bruised and bewildered by the fast-escalating developments, Russell stared round dazedly.

'I tell you, I'm innocent.'

A backhander from a citizen rocked his head.

'Shut your murdering mouth. All murderers claim they're innocent. We don't need scum like you in Elsinburg. You killed a good man and his wife. Now you'll pay the price.'

Again the stables yielded up the means of execution. A rangy gelding was led out, jerking nervously on the head harness as it was exposed to the volatile ferment of the mob.

Eager hands pushed the noose around Russell's neck. He was still fighting the mob but with limited success. He was helpless against the numerous and excited bodies pressing around him, each one eager to be the one to fit the noose. Again, there was no shortage of help to lift him onto the horse's back. A loud cheer went up as he was raised up above the level of the crowd.

'Let this be a warning to all murderers in Elsinburg.'

'Elsinburg justice is swift an' sure.'

'Hang on, hang on,' someone shouted from the mob.

'That's just what we're doin',' came the answer.

Laughter erupted from sections of the crowd. Those that had been drinking heavily were the most vociferous and were pressing close to get a good view of the execution.

'I mean the kid might wanna say a prayer or something. Surely he'll wanna make peace with his maker.'

Through the mist of pain and despair Russell thought there was something familiar about the voice.

'I know young Dane. I rode the trail with him. He's a God-fearing man.' It was Mathew Maxwell calling out for the compassionate behaviour.

'That's right, I know he'd wanna say his prayers,' enjoined his brother, Francis. 'Let's bow our heads in respect. If the fella hasta go, let him go in God's grace.'

It was the right ploy. The men eager for the swift execution hung back.

'Hell, why not? Give him the break that he didn't give Paul Lynas and Marian.'

'Fella, you got anything to say to your Maker before we send you to hell?'

This brought more laughter. It was a nervous laughter. The talk of God and prayer was making some among the crowd uneasy.

Russell searched amongst the crowd for his friends. He caught sight of Francis Maxwell. The youngster was mouthing silent instructions to Russell but he could not make out what the signals meant. Then Francis joined his hands together in an attitude of prayer and cast his eyes upwards. Not knowing quite what was expected of him Russell decided to comply with his friend's instructions.

'Let God be my witness this day that I am innocent of the crime I am accused of. I go to meet my Maker with a clear conscience,' he began in a loud voice. 'When I enter in heaven's gate my soul is pure as driven snow.' He risked a glance at his friend. Francis was nodding vigorously. Closing his eyes he continued. 'God take me into your bosom. I have walked the good path. I have fought the

74

good fight. My life is behind me but I give it into your forgiving hands.'

Russell was babbling on, desperately racking his brain for inspiration. He had never been interested in religion but he knew the more he prayed the longer he postponed his hanging. Somehow he had a notion that the Maxwell brothers were playing for time. So he struggled on, his rambling prayer becoming more and more fanciful.

A bearded man lurched forward. He was the one Russell had injured with his cuffs. There was blood on his face.

'The hell with this, we ain't got time for this holy nonsense.'

He slapped the roan hard across the rump with his hand. The horse jumped forward taking everyone by surprise. Russell's praying was abruptly cut off as the horse went from under him and the noose tightened round his neck. Then he was swinging wildly underneath the tree. The world was spinning around him and the rope began to squeeze the life out of him.

18

Francis Maxwell plunged forward through the crowd. His one thought was to save his friend. He arrived beneath the booted feet and reaching out his hands he managed to stabilize the hanging man. Once he had hold of the boots he pushed up, taking the weight of his friend. There were angry shouts and someone kicked him in the thigh.

'Goddamn you,' Francis shrieked.

Suddenly his brother was by his side. Mathew had his sixgun out and was brandishing it before him.

'Stop them goddamn cowboys,' someone shouted from the crowd.

'Anyone tries to stop us, we'll shoot,' Mathew yelled.

He levelled his pistol at the mob. The crowd fell back from the brothers. Francis was wobbling dangerously as he attempted to balance his friend on his shoulders.

Suddenly a shot rang out and Francis cried out and fell away from the hanging Russell. He was clutching his shoulder. Blood seeped from between his fingers.

'Goddamn murdering bastards!'

Mathew pointed his pistol and pulled the trigger. He was indifferent as to whom he hit. There was a general scattering of bodies from around the scene of the hanging. Mathew looked over his shoulder in despair at the dangling legs of his friend.

'Francis, are you hurt bad? Here take this pistol and shoot anyone as comes near. I'll try to help Russell.'

Francis got to his feet and grabbed hold of the gun. His face was twisted in pain as he pointed it at the cowering citizens.

'I'll shoot every goddamn one of you,' he screamed at them.

A shot came whistling towards him and missed. Francis fired instinctively. Behind him Mathew was juggling with Russell, trying to keep the youth from strangling. Suddenly the air was filled with the noise of several weapons firing. The brothers looked up in despair. Horses were bearing down on the crowd. The men atop the racing horses were firing off pistols. Most of the shots were going over the heads of the mob. The Maxwells watched in relief as their brother rode into the fray with cowboys from the Dane ranch.

Already demoralized by the defiant stand of the Maxwell brothers, this new attack was too much for the mob. They broke and ran. Into the space vacated by the mob came the riders led by Clive Dane. They pulled up in a cloud of dust.

Clive Dane wasted no time. He was straining forward, standing on his stirrups. With a long bowie he hacked at the rope around his nephew's neck. The rope parted and Russell dropped awkwardly to the ground. Bernard Maxwell was off his horse and ministering to the comatose youth. His brothers gathered round, anxiously watching Bernard as he pulled the remains of the rope from around Russell's neck.

'Keep your guns on those lily-livered scum that can hang a helpless kid but scurry for home at the sound of gunfire,' Clive Dane snarled.

In obedience to his instructions, the two Texans he had brought along for support ranged their horses forward and kept watch on the street.

'Sure boss, you can rely on us.'

'Nothing like a hole in a fella's head to stop him taking interest in anyone else's business.'

The two hard-faced gunmen sat their horses easy and gazed around the area with flint-hard stares. They need not have worried. The mob had had enough. Hanging a helpless boy was easy. Facing up to a gang of cowboys slinging lead around was not their idea of entertainment. The street cleared.

'How is he?' Clive Dane asked the Maxwell brothers.

'He's still alive, Mr Dane. You got here just in the nick of time.'

'Looks like you boys had it all in hand afore we got

77

here. Mrs Dane'll sure wanna thank you boys for saving her son.'

'Hell, Mr Dane, if you hadn't arrived when you did I reckon Russell and my brother and me would all be finished.'

'Get a buggy from the livery. We'll take Russell back to the ranch. And hurry up about it, afore these pasty-faced townsfolk bolster up on their courage with some John Barleycorn and try an' take Russell again.'

As it was, they made it out of Elsinburg without incident. The unconscious Russell and the wounded Francis Maxwell were in the buggy. Riding shotgun were Bernard and Mathew Maxwell, Clive Dane and his Texas gunmen.

Russell came to as he was carried into his home. He looked around him with a dazed expression. His mother was supervising his transfer from the buggy to the house.

'Careful. Carry him into the living room. Thank you everyone, I'm so grateful.' Then she noticed the blood on the younger of the Maxwells. 'Francis, are you hurt? How did that happen?'

'Oh, it ain't nothing, ma'am. Just a scratch.'

'Take no notice of him, Gertrude. It was him and Mathew as rescued Russell,' called out Clive. 'He was shot because he was trying to save him. Take him inside and have someone take care of that shoulder.'

The last thing Russell remembered was the sudden choking as the rope tightened round his neck. Now he was being carried in to his home.

'Mother,' he croaked.

'You're safe now, son. Clive and your friends brought you back home. I'll take care of you.'

Russell relaxed and allowed himself to be ferried

78

inside. He lay on a couch while his mother fussed over him. Gradually he felt his strength return.

'What can I get you, son?'

'I guess a drink would be mighty welcome,' he whispered, unable to use his voice to its full extent. He imagined he could still feel the tight constriction of the rope around his neck.

'What would you like – coffee?'

'A bourbon would be better.'

Gertrude Dane pressed her lips together in disapproval but did not voice her objections. At that moment Nathan Jessop arrived carrying a small case. Because of his skill with doctoring animals, Nathan was also called upon to tender to the human injured. The healer eyed Francis sitting with a bloody pad held against his shoulder. Then he turned his attention to Russell, now sitting up.

'Who do you want me to see to first, Mrs Dane?' he asked.

For the first time Russell noticed the pale form of his friend.

'Francis, what the hell happened to you?'

Before the youth could answer, Mrs Dane answered for him. 'From what I can make out he got shot trying to keep you safe.'

Russell immediately looked contrite. 'Damnit to hell, Francis, I sure am sorry.'

He got a wan smile from the injured cowboy. 'Hell Russell, you'da done the same for me anytime.'

'See to Francis first, Nathan. All I got is a sore throat,' Russell said.

With a glass of bourbon in his hand, Russell lay back and went over in his mind all that had happened. What he could not figure was his Uncle Clive coming to his rescue.

Then the person he was thinking about arrived in the room. Russell watched as his mother rushed to his uncle's side and embraced him.

'Oh Clive, how can I ever thank you for saving these boys?'

How she hangs around his neck, Russell thought. And why did he save me?

His uncle smiled over his mother's shoulder at Russell and winked.

19

'I tell you Gertrude, he'll have to go away for a while. At least till this blows over. Killing a sheriff is bad medicine. And they won't be able to arrest him if they don't know where he's at. We can tell the authorities he's gone into hiding for his own safety. Hopefully they'll understand that after the lynching. We can always say he'll come forward when a formal charge has been laid and a proper investigation into the shooting had been put in place. In the meantime we'll hire our own investigator. But Russell mustn't be about while things are so hot.'

'Oh Clive, but where would he go?'

'Can't he go back to the academy?'

'He seems dead set against returning. There was some bother over a duel with young Forten. If you remember, Charlie shot Forten the elder and it seems the son wants to even the score.'

'Yeah, I heard about that fracas. Who'da thought his kid would come along seeking vengeance?' Clive pursed his lips in thought. 'We'll just hav'ta send him down to

Texas. I have friends down there'll take care of him.'

'He's only a boy, Clive. He can't go all that way on his own.'

'Tell you what – those two Texans as just joined us are two good men – Rod Krantz and Gill Stern. You shoulda seen how they rode in with us and held off those towns-folk. They ain't scared of anyone or anything. We'll send them with Russell. Their job will be to protect him and guide him down in Texas. He'll be safe with them and outta the way of the law till we sort this mess out.'

Gertrude Dane's face frowned in quiet concern as she contemplated Clive Dane's solution.

'I guess you're right, Clive. I hate to see him go but after what happened there seems no other way. I just can't understand how he came to be mixed up with Paul Lynas. When I asked him what he was doing at their house he hedges around the whole thing. Says as how he went to see Paul to ask him what he should do about Forten spreading lies about him being a coward. Then the shooting started and when it was all over Paul and Marian Lynas were lying dead. Oh, Clive, it's all too much for me.'

'Don't worry, Gertrude. What say we get married as soon as Russell is safely on his way? At least when he comes back he'll know he's coming back to a stable home.'

The couple moved together and embraced.

'Clive, you've been so supportive during this time of trouble. But I couldn't think of a wedding till I know Russell is safe.'

He chucked her under the chin and smiled down at her worried face. 'Don't you worry your little head about Russell. He'll be safe with my men riding shotgun.'

She hugged him tight and felt very, very safe in his arms.

One by one, Russell shook hands with the Maxwell brothers.

'Don't you want us with you, Russell?'

'Hell no! You boys done enough for me. No one could ask for better friends. I'm going on the run from the law. If you boys come with me you'll guilty by association.'

'Where you going anyway?'

'It's secret. That way nobody can tell anything. I'll just disappear and when this all blows over I'll come back and we'll paint that ole town of Elsinburg red.'

'Hell, Russell, they near as damnit painted the town red with our blood. Right now the boss says as Elsinburg is out of bounds. I'd sure like to go in there and shoot the hell outta that there goddamn town.'

'Yeah, they sure had us treed for a while. Only for you boys I'd be dangling on that tree like rotting fruit.'

Again they shook hands and Russell walked to his horse. It was being held by one of the Texans who were to accompany him on his travels. Russell swung into the saddle and waved to his friends. They stood morosely watching him as he rode up towards the house. The Texans waited a respectable distance behind. His mother was on the porch. Clive stood behind her.

'Oh Russell,' his mother said tearfully. 'Please take care. I'll count the days till you come back.'

'I'll be all right, mother. I got these milkmaids here to watch over me.' He nodded recognition to Clive. 'Uncle Clive, thanks for all you done.'

'Russell, you're like a son to me – the son I never had. Just you take care. Soon as I have this mess cleared up we'll send for you.'

With a wave of his hand, Russell tugged his mount around and headed for the road. His mother kept waving till he was out of sight.

Russell rode away with leaden feelings. It was as if everything that had happened to him over the last few days had happened to someone else. He was still hazy over the events in the Lynas household. True, he had been drinking with his friend Horace and that had not helped clear thinking. He was still fairly certain Sheriff Lynas had meant to kill him.

According to Marian's original story her husband and Clive Dane had murdered his father. Then she had lured him back to the house to tell him the sheriff wasn't involved. To compound everything his Uncle Clive had ridden into Elsinburg to rescue him. If his uncle had indeed been guilty of murdering his father, why had he risked coming into town to rescue the murdered man's son? Surely the right course would have been to let the people of Elsinburg hang him. That way a troublesome nephew would be put out of the way without any risk to himself. He shook his head as if the sudden movement would clear his head.

Whether Marian Lynas was telling the truth or not it would now be impossible to establish. With Sheriff Lynas dead, he had nothing but the story Marian had told him. His head was going round and round in circles as he tried to think logically about the mystery.

'The hell with it,' he muttered.

If his Uncle Clive was involved in the death of his father and wanted it concealed, he was going about it in a peculiar way. By saving his nephew he was protecting the only person who suspected him.

The trio rode steadily. They had many miles to ride before reaching Texas.

20

Russell found the Texans entertaining travelling companions. When they stopped for meal breaks or overnight stops the pair regaled the youngster with yarns of Texas life. They had worked as cowhands for a while and told him tall tales of hazardous roundups. They made out that wild longhorns were more dangerous than mountain lions when on a cattle drive.

'Yessiree, I seen cowboys speared on the end of a horn. Maybe take days to die. The wound would fester and go mouldy. Terrible thing to see a man go rotten afore your very eyes – terrible.'

'Even more terrible for the fella as is going rotten,' Russell suggested. He suspected his minders were setting out to worry him with their talk of the dangers of the Texan longhorn, but he took it all in good heart.

'Once seen a fella trampled by a stampede. By the time we shovelled up his bits and rolled him in a slicker the remains was hardly any thicker than a whiskey bottle.'

'How'd you bury him?' Russell asked innocently. 'I guess the best way would be to bore a hole in the ground and slip the rolled up slicker into that.'

'Terrible thing to see men die on the trail.'

If their tales of death were designed to trouble the youngster, they failed. The sudden and violent deaths of Sheriff Lynas and his wife had inured Russell to violence. The suspicion that his father had been murdered by his uncle, coupled with the attempted lynching, had also toughened him to the cruelty of his fellows. So a few hairy tales of death on the cow trails fazed him not at all.

84

After several days riding, the travellers decided to stop over in a town called Dartsville and take a break from travelling. All three were in agreement they should try to exchange their mounts for fresh ones.

It was a typically Western town with false-fronted buildings standing like jaded ladies among new stores in course of construction. There were the usual taverns and saloons and eating-houses. Partway along the front they passed the sheriff's office. A large corpulent man with a badge on his bulging shirt came out as they rode past. He stepped into the street and purposely followed the three riders.

With common agreement the trio pulled up at the Golden Arrow – a large gaudy building with painted signs advertising the best whiskey, the best games and the best girls in town. Wearily they dismounted and were tying up when the sheriff drew level with them. Russell glanced nervously at the law officer from under lowered eyebrows.

'Howdy fellas, where you from?'

'Waal, originally we're from Texas,' drawled Rod Krantz. 'Where're you from yourself, Sheriff?'

'Are you passing through or staying?' the sheriff asked, ignoring Rod's question.

'Waal that all depends, if'n the likker's good and the girls are friendly we might stay a night or two.'

The law officer eyed up the three men and noted the tied-down holsters worn by the Texans.

'Sheriff Belson's my name.' The law officer put a large hand on the polished butt of his holstered Colt and stared meaningfully at the strangers. 'I run a peaceable town. If there's any trouble I shoot first and ask questions later.'

'Understood, officer. We ain't here looking for trouble. Just a day, mebby two then we're on our way.'

Tipping his hat, Rod turned and nodded to his

companions. All three walked inside the saloon conscious of the big man watching them.

Inside the dim-lit saloon Russell found he was sweating. He was remembering his last brush with the law and the almost fatal consequences.

'Goddamn big-mouthed sheriff,' muttered Gill Stern, who had remained silent during the exchange, as had Russell. 'What the hell's he mean hassling us like that? It's a goddamn free country. A man can stop in a town as long as he wants without some fat-assed buffoon asking damn-fool questions.'

'Hush your mouth, Gill. Don't forget we're on a mission.'

Rod Krantz nodded his head towards Russell. Both men looked at the youth then glanced sharply back at each other. A meaningful look passed between them.

'Sure, Rod, you're right. We gotta look after the kid.'

Gill Stern suddenly giggled – his good humour returning. He punched his friend lightly in the chest and, smirking broadly, the Texans moved each side of Russell and escorted him to the bar.

'Come on kid, we'll show you how us Texans have a good time.'

'What about the horses?'

'Just a couple of drinks to sample the likker and wash out the trail dust. Then we'll mosey down the livery. After that, it's a big thick steak with potatoes an' gravy. That'll set us up for some real drinking.'

That was the plan and that was what they did. Russell marvelled at the amount of money the cowboys had to throw around. At the livery they paid to have their mounts unsaddled, fed and watered and stabled for the night. They would negotiate for fresh mounts the next day.

The eating-house fed the cowboys with the biggest steaks on the menu followed by pie and fresh cream. Back at the Golden Arrow they each purchased a bottle of Abraham's whiskey – the best in the house. Carrying the bottles with their glasses, the cowboys found an unoccupied table and sat down to do some serious drinking.

Russell's mother had insisted on giving him a money belt stuffed with dollars. He had decided to use the money sparingly as he did not know how long it had to last but he need not have worried. His travelling companions seemed to have plenty to spend. Briefly he wondered how two ordinary cowpokes had so much wealth, but it was no concern of his. For the moment he could drink and forget the last few weeks. Weeks that had turned his world upside down.

The Texans laughed and joshed him and encouraged him to drink up. Russell needed no urging. He was happy to drink himself into oblivion and forgetfulness.

'Here's to good friends,' he toasted.

The friends looked at each other, burst into laughter and joined him in his toast.

'Here's to good friends,' they chorused.

The levels in the Abraham's whiskey bottles steadily lowered.

21

'Oooh!'

Russell held his head and moaned softly. It seemed to him that the longhorns his Texan companions had been telling him about had trampled all over his head. One was trapped inside his skull and was rampaging around trying to affect an escape. Slowly he prised his eyelids open.

'I ain't ever gonna touch another drop of whiskey in my life,' he intoned softly. He had vague memories of similar sentiments expressed sometime in a past life.

The place was in darkness. He lay where he was, afraid to stir in case the mad bumping in his head might get worse. For long moments he contemplated his situation. Slowly recollection came.

'Goddamn Texans can sure pack away the whiskey.'

Careful not to move sudden he tried to sit up. In spite of the dark his head spun dizzily. Little lights imploded inside his skull. He rested, feeling a sour sickness in his stomach.

He figured he was in the saloon.

Girls. He remembered the girls. They joined them at the table. For the life of him he couldn't remember their faces. They smelt of cheap scent and booze. Their lips were passionate red with powdered breasts that oozed from bodice tops. They seemed able to drink as much as the men.

Briefly he wondered what the time was. By the pitch darkness engulfing him he judged it was deep into the night. He remembered the money belt and anxiously felt his middle. He breathed a sigh of relief as he patted the rounded swelling of the pockets. Slowly the sounds of the night established themselves. He heard a woman's laughter and the low mumble of a man's voice.

Did he have a place to sleep? He had vague memories of booking a room.

'Goddamn it, what the hell am I doing lying on this saloon floor like the town drunk?'

Anxious not to set his aching head off again, he gingerly climbed to his feet. He felt the hard edge of a table and held on to it while the room swayed around him. Waves of nausea rose in him and involuntarily his guts heaved. Helplessly he bent over the table and emptied his stomach onto the surface. With shaking hand, he wiped his lips.

Bed. That's what he needed – a bed. Somewhere upstairs a bed was waiting. He groped his way to the stairway and, feeling the boards with his hands, slowly he mounted. Each step was a giddy increase of the spinning inside his head. The landing flattened out before him. He was slowly gaining some night-sight. A row of doors stretched out before him.

'Goddamn it, have I any idea which room I'm supposed to be in?'

A woman's laughter pealed out again and a man's low rumbling voice could be heard. That gave him an idea. He went to the nearest door and pressed his ear against it. After a minute he could detect gentle snoring. From down the hallway the woman laughed again. Intrigued, Russell tiptoed along the carpeted hall and stopped at the room he believed the laughter was coming from.

'I tell you I'm well-heeled.'

Russell was sure he detected the Texas drawl of one of his companions. He sighed with relief. If it was Rod or Gill they would put him right as to which room was his.

'You cowboys are allas spinnin' a gal a tale.'

'I tell you we got paid to do a job. We got half up-front and the other half when we complete the job.'

The girl laughed again. 'What sorta job? You looking after that kid downstairs as passed out?'

'Sorta. Here, hand me the makings.'

There was a pause. Russell leaned against the panels of the door, intrigued with the talk going on inside. He was in no doubt he was the kid the woman spoke about.

'You don't strike me as the type to act as nursemaid to no wet-assed kid.'

'That ain't no wet-assed kid down there. Now don't breathe a word of what I'm tellin' you. That kid down there has killed a sheriff and his wife in their own home. He's on the run an' we gotta take care of him.'

'Never! You mean he's a murderer. Laws amighty, what if he starts akilling around here!'

'Aw, don't you worry your pretty little head about no kid. Ole Gill Stern'll take care of him.'

'Is that the job you telling me about?'

Then Stern laughed. It was a cold, cynical sound. 'We gotta take care of him all right. His uncle paid us. Told us the kid hasta meet with an accident. He don't want him comin' back an' claimin' his share of the ranch.'

'You mean his uncle wants him killed then after that he gets to own the ranch?'

'Well, not quite. He hasta marry the rich widder as owns the ranch – the kid's mother. We gotta go back with a sad tale of how the kid met his end an' we get paid the other half of our fee. What's that?'

'What's what? I ain't heard anything.'

'I thought I heard something outside the door.'

Russell had slumped against the wall, his head spinning worse now that he had overheard the dreadful details of the plot against him. Inside the room the bedsprings creaked.

'I'll take a look-see.'

Russell stumbled across the landing to the head of the stairs. He grabbed for the stair-post as he placed his foot on the top step and missed. Desperately he scrabbled for

a grip. His feet slipped from underneath him. With a sick-
ening sensation he plummeted down the stairway, seem-
ingly hitting each step on the way down. Above him a light
leaked onto the landing as a door opened.

Gill Stern poked his head round the door. Cautiously
he stepped out on the landing. In one hand he held a
pistol. He walked to the top of the stairs. For a moment he
peered into the darkness that was the stairwell.

'What the goddamn hell's goin' on? Anyone there?'

Silence had settled like a blanket over the saloon.

'Goddamn drunks,' Gill Stern muttered.

He turned and walked back into the room again. The
door closed behind him and once again the landing was in
darkness.

At the foot of the stair, Russell lay bruised and dazed.
His head was a muddle of confused thoughts. The alcohol
he had consumed in the course of the night was not helping settle anything. Painfully he sat up and leaned against
a banister rail.

Gill Stern and Rod Krantz, who were supposed to guide
him on his journey to Texas, had been paid by his uncle to
kill him. His mother would never know what had
happened to her only son. She would marry her brother-
in-law and live the rest of her life with the man whose
hands were stained with the blood of her family.

Gill Stern scratched contentedly as he stepped downstairs
after his night of ardour with his paid companion. His

Texan partner was waiting for him.

'Let's go get some breakfast.'

'Where the hell's that damn kid?'

'More 'an likely still flat out in his room. I think he was under the table when I left him.'

The men smirked knowingly at each other.

'Some tough kid, eh, thinkin' he could out-drink us.'

They left the saloon and headed for the eating-house. Inside, as they sat down at a table, they noticed the sheriff. He was at a table with an empty, greasy plate in front of him and sipping from a steaming mug. The lawman frowned across at them. Both men gave him hard stares in return.

'Thought you fellas mighta left with your friend.'

The waitress approached the Texans' table, but they ignored her. They were staring intently at the sheriff.

'What the hell you mean?'

'That kid pulled out sometime last night. Liveryman came in, said his hoss was gone. You fellas plan on stayin' on much longer?'

'Hell!' Stern exploded.

Both men pushed back their chairs and strode from the diner. The sheriff stared after them with a puzzled look on his face.

'Them fellas seem a mite upset,' the lawman mused aloud.

'Sheriff, what the hell you doin' chasin' off my customers?' the waitress complained.

They found the liveryman working at his chores. He peered at them with narrowed eyes – his wrinkled face and untidy clothes giving a reasonably good impression of a crow-scarer.

'Pulled out last night sometime. Weren't no one here to see him go. Saddled up his hoss and went.'

The Texans swore long and luridly.

'Any idea what direction he went?' Stern asked when they paused for breath.

'When I was comin' in this mornin', I saw tracks headin' south on the Colston trail.'

'You think it was him?'

'Every hoss that comes in this here livery has his own sign in his hoofs. I kin tell every hoss as it comes and goes. Yeah, it were your friend, all right.' The old man spat onto the floor. 'You fellas payin' for his stay? He never settled up afore he went.'

'Damn that kid, what the hell he up and run for?'

The two men eyed each other.

'You don't think he suspects somethin'?'

'Hell, I don't see how he can. Nobody said nothin'.'

'We'd better hightail it after him otherwise we kiss goodbye to the rest of that there money.'

'What about breakfast?' queried Stern.

Krantz turned a mean eye to his friend.

'Breakfast'll hav'ta wait. We're goin' after that kid.'

Russell was lost. He gazed around him at the unrelenting terrain. Ahead lay an oak thicket he was sure he had passed earlier. A thin stream meandered into the canyon he could see on his right.

'I ain't sure but that there bunch of oaks and that there stream looks damn familiar.'

When he had left so abruptly during the night he had not thought to take a fresh mount. Still suffering from the effects of alcohol indulgence and the frightening tumble down the stairs, his only thought had been to get away.

Hurriedly he had saddled up and grabbed his kit from where the liveryman had stored it. As he worked he kept looking over his shoulder thinking any moment Gill Stern and Rod Krantz, his uncle's hired killers, were behind him. He had walked the horse till he was beyond the boundaries of the town before urging it to gallop at speed away from Dartsville and his dangerous travelling companions.

Now, both he and his horse, neither recovered from the ordeal of several days' travelling, were worn-out and lost. He gazed around him despondently.

'Hell, there's water here and firewood. I'll stop and camp somewhere around here. If I'm lost then I guess them killers won't find me neither.'

With a sigh, he turned his tired horse towards the canyon. Plentiful sage along with scant growth of oak and piñon grew beneath the rugged walls of the canyon. He pushed on and on inside the towering walls and eventually the floor of the valley broadened out. Oak grew more plentiful in the broad stretches that were opening out before him. His horse stumbled. He reached down and patted its neck.

'I guess we're both done in, fella. We'll stop and rest awhile.'

He guided the tired mount into a stand of trees. Dismounting, he unsaddled and left the horse to forage for itself. Surprisingly he was hungry. He searched the saddlebags but found nothing to eat.

'Hell, no need for Rod Krantz and Gill Stern to finish me – I'll just starve to death.'

Finding a level place beneath the trees, he spread his blanket and stretched out. Moodily he stared up at the tracery of foliage and reflected on his plight.

'I guess them fellas will wanna earn their bonus. I reckon they'll come after me. I'll just have to keep pushing on and hope to reach civilization sometime.'

He could hear his horse moving further and further

94

away in its search for grass. Tiredness overwhelmed him and within minutes he was fast asleep.

'Get his weapons.'

Rough hands were pulling at his gun belt. Suddenly he was awake.

He snapped his eyes open. The outlines of a hard face filled his vision. He threw a punch. It was instinctive and hard. With a curse, the face disappeared. Russell crabbed his hand towards his gun. Then his head jerked violently sideways as a boot cannoned into his ear. Desperately he tried to roll away. There was an agonizing pain in his side as another boot crashed into his ribs. His breath was driven from his lungs with the brutal suddenness of the blow. Gasping for breath, he rolled onto his back. Then the boot was in his throat and he was staring up at the snarling countenance of Rod Krantz. The nozzle of a Colt was aimed into his face.

'Had enough kid, or do I finish you now?'

Russell lay gasping for breath as the boot pressed into his throat partially cutting off his wind. He grabbed the boot and twisted hard. There was a harsh sound from Krantz. The dark hole of the Colt moved fractionally and he pulled the trigger.

The blast of the shot so close stunned Russell and momentarily he stopped struggling. The bullet buried itself in the dirt near his head. He flopped back and went still. The boot was removed from his throat and he sucked air into his lungs. He massaged his bruised neck as he stared up at the two men who had tracked him down so easily.

'Goddamn no-good kid.'

Gill Stern kicked the helpless youngster as he rubbed his jaw where Russell had hit him on first awakening. Rod Krantz, still holding his Colt, squatted down beside their captive.

'Why'd you light out without us, kid? I thought we were all buddies – ridin' the trail together. How we supposed to take care of you if 'n you go off like this on your own?'

'Yeah,' Russell said bitterly, 'you were to take care of me, all right.'

Krantz frowned. 'What you mean?'

Russell shot a glance at Gill Stern glaring back balefully at him. 'I heard him telling his whore how my uncle paid you to make sure I never came back from this trip. You think I'd hang about and make things easy for you?'

Rod Krantz glanced sideways at his partner. 'You crud, Gill! What a goddamn, dumb-ass play that was!'

'He's lyin'. I never told no one nothin'.'

Krantz looked in disgust at his partner. 'How the hell he know to make a run for it?'

'Hell, what's it matter? We gotta do the job sometime. It's no picnic playin' nursemaid to no wet-assed kid anyhow.'

'I guess.'

Krantz cocked his pistol and pointed it at Russell. Still lying on his back, the youngster stared back in disbelief at the Texan.

'You can't. . . .'

Whatever else he wanted to say was lost as the Colt roared out for the second time in a few minutes. The shot echoed around the canyon, gradually fading as the noise was absorbed in its ancient walls.

Elias Carter was a moody character. At times dark and brooding while at other times boisterous and playful.

Today he was brooding on a failed bank robbery as he rode towards his hideout.

The target for the bank job was a town in southwest Missouri. Somehow the citizens of the town had gotten wind of the robbery and a reception committee was organized to fight off the raiders. The result was two men dead and empty saddlebags.

His gang were strung out behind him. They rode as individuals, for Elias had this theory that if his men were ambushed most would survive or be able to strike back as they came up on the scene of any attack.

As well as that, gangs of horsemen might attract unwelcome attention from lawmen. The theory had never been put into practice for the gang had never been ambushed. Paradoxically it was for that reason Carter believed his strategy was right.

The gang leader turned into the canyon that held the large caves in which his men rested up between raids. He wasn't in a hurry. There was nothing to hurry back for. Till the next job, all he had to look forward to were the recriminations of his fellow outlaws as they chewed over the failure to put their hands on some stolen cash.

The shot, when it came, jerked him out of his self-pity. He drew rein and sat for a while scanning ahead. Nothing moved. Cautiously he nudged his horse forward. The second shot followed close behind the first. Elias Carter rode more cautiously now.

Carter's dark moods were suited to his appearance. No matter how close or how often he shaved, dark shadow of a beard persisted on his lower face. That face was oval shaped. A cleft chin and a flattened nose gave him an outward show of suppressed violence. This was true for, if provoked, Elias Carter could explode in instant and violent action.

As he came in sight of a grove of oaks he saw a saddled horse grazing on the sparse grass growing by the side of the trail. Just then two riders emerged from the trees. They did not notice Elias and he sat his horse and watched as the men caught up the reins of the spare horse. They draped a gun belt over the pommel and stuffed some belongings into the saddlebags. Finished stowing the goods, they turned and began jogging towards him.

Elias slid a spare pistol from his saddlebag and held it on his horse's neck. The horse's mane concealed the weapon. Elias awaited developments. He was curious what two riders were doing so close to his hideout and also he was curious about the gunshots and the spare horse.

Rod Krantz and Gill Stern saw the rider waiting on the trail ahead of them. They halted and conferred. Then, loosening the guns in their holsters, they jogged nearer. Elias waited, immobile.

'Howdy fella,' one of the Texan's drawled as they approached. 'You waitin' for someone?'

'Yeah, I was waiting for you fellas. Heard some shots and kinda wondered what was happening.'

The strangers shot a sideways glance at each other.

'Oh that. We was fixin' to shoot us a rabbit for supper. Dang well missed the little fella. One lucky rabbit – two unlucky Texans.'

They began to edge their horses obviously intending to pass by.

'I see you got a spare rig there. Where's the fella as is riding that?'

'You ask too many questions, fella. Just move aside and we'll be on our way.'

Elias shook his head. 'Uh-huh, you're right. I do ask questions. I also like answers. My guess is there's some

98

poor fella lying in those trees with a piece of lead in him.'

'You're playing a dangerous game here, fella. Just move aside. That's twice I asked. I won't ask a third time.'

The Texans began edging their mounts apart. Hands slid onto their thighs – a sure sign they were prepared to go for their holstered weapons. Elias pursed his lips.

'Tell you what, let's all ride back and see what lies within those trees. That way I get to find out what you were shooting at and satisfy myself you fellas weren't lying to me.'

'Mister,' Rod Krantz said in a dangerously low voice, 'you wanna die out here in this lonely place? Cause you're goin' about it the right way.'

'Yeah, bigmouth, there's two of us and, in case you hadn't noticed, there's only one of you,' Gill Stern interjected.

Both riders went very still and Elias watched their gazes slide past him. He had no doubt what had distracted the two men. Some of his men would be riding up the trail.

'Is that a fact?' Elias enjoined affably.

Rod Krantz and Gill Stern watched as a rider approached. Elias sat where he was, waiting.

'Elias, anything wrong?' It was Myron Holly, a serious-looking man with dark, brooding eyes. He drew alongside his chief and waited.

'Myron, ride up into that clump of trees and see what's in there.'

'Hell, fella, there's no need,' exclaimed Krantz. 'We'll satisfy your curiosity. There's a dead fella lyin' in there.'

But Holly was already past and entering the trees.

'Why'd you kill him?'

'He's a wanted man. There's a bounty on him.'

'What'd he do?'

'Hell, he killed a sheriff and his wife.'

99

'Killed a sheriff,' mused Elias.

Holly came out of the trees. 'There's a dead kid in here.'

'A kid?' queried Elias.

The Texans remained silent.

'You bounty hunters?' asked Elias.

Something lightened in Gill Stem's face. 'Sure, that's it. We're bounty hunters. We're gonna collect the reward on that killer.'

'How you gonna prove you killed him with no body?'

What Elias observed was true. Bounty hunters needed a body to be identified before receiving their reward.

'We . . . we brung along his effects. He's wanted up in Elsinburg – too far to drag a dead body.'

Elias steadily regarded the two men.

'Hell, Elias,' Myron Holly called. 'If they're bounty hunters, shoot them. One day they might come after us.'

24

Elias knew when the decision was made between the men that they were going to shoot their way out of this fix. Even as Rod Krantz went for his pistol Elias was bringing up his own weapon from where he had hidden it in the horse's mane. His first shot hit the bounty hunter in the arm.

Krantz was cursing as he brought up his Colt. He let off two shots but his horse was dancing sideways and his bullets went well wide of their target. Suddenly he grunted and bent over his horse's neck as Myron Holly's shot took him in the side. He tried to swivel to shoot at this new threat but Holly shot again and hit the Texan in the head.

Rod Krantz was dead before he hit the ground.

Gill Stem lasted a little longer. He managed to get off a shot that buzzed past the outlaw chief's ear. His second shot went up in the air as Elias pumped two shots into his chest. Badly wounded but still holding onto his pistol, he plummeted to the ground. Desperately, he fired from under his horse. The shot hit Elias's horse in the rear, causing it to jerk and plunge in pain and fear. It took all of Elias's strength and riding skill to stay on board his wounded horse. Preoccupied as he was holding onto his madly plunging horse, Elias was unable to fire back at the man on the ground. Because Krantz's horse obscured his view, Myron Holly couldn't fire at the wounded bounty hunter.

While all this was going on, the rest of the gang had ridden up and were watching developments. Seeing Elias and Myron in trouble, they decided to take a hand. Snatching out their weapons and whooping loudly, they raced to circle around the downed bounty hunter. Gill Stem stood no chance as bullets came in from all directions. He twitched and jerked as bullets riddled his body. Still yelling and shooting, the gang turned their attention to the other dead bounty hunter and treated him to the same barrage.

'Stop firing! For God's sake, stop firing!'

Elias was yelling at his wildly shooting gang. The firing petered out.

'What's the matter with you guys? You think bullets grow on trees?'

'We thought you was in trouble, Elias, that's all.'

'Sure, Elias, I reckon we sorta saved your life comin' on like we did.'

'What – shootin' fellas as is already dead!' Elias replied scornfully.

But the outlaws were not to be suppressed. The little

fracas had livened up their day.

'Think you're losin' your touch, Elias,' observed a squint-eyed man with a mean face. 'First a botched bank job and now almost killed by these bounty hunters.'

'Ichabod Goodyear, you think you could do any better?'

Elias was staring malevolently at his tormentor. He inched his wounded horse, now calmed down, closer to the outspoken outlaw. For a moment Goodyear held his gaze, then he averted his eyes and was silent.

'Drag these fellas into those trees. We'll hav'ta bury them. Can't have dead bodies attracting attention.'

They searched the dead bounty hunters and were surprised at the money the men were carrying.

'Damnit, maybe bounty hunting's better than outlawing. These fellas surely are well heeled.'

As the outlaws were marvelling at the apparent wealth of the men they had killed, Myron Holly called out.

'Elias, this fella back in the trees ain't dead.'

They gathered round, staring curiously at the still figure lying amidst the fallen leaves.

'Damnit, he's only a kid.'

Myron Holly was kneeling beside the wounded man. He looked up at Elias. 'What you reckon, boss? Think we should take him with us?'

Elias took in the dark stain on the boy's chest. 'You think he'll survive?'

'Dunno, Elias, sure looks in a pretty bad way.'

'Mmm . . . those bounty hunters said as he killed a sheriff and was on the run. If 'n he's one of us, then mebby we oughta try and save him.' Suddenly he came to a decision. 'Get the boys to rig up a stretcher from some branches and blankets. We'll take him back with us. If he lives he lives, if he dies he dies.'

The outlaws set to work to make a crude stretcher. They hacked down long straight oak branches and trimmed them. Using rawhide they made fast two blankets that they stretched between the poles. This construction was slung between the mounts of the two dead bounty hunters.

For men who had just pumped several pounds of lead into the two bounty hunters, the outlaws were surprisingly gentle with the injured Russell. While all this was going on the rest of the gang were digging a hole to bury the dead Texans.

In just over an hour from the first shot fired at Russell, the convoy got underway. Myron Holly took responsibility for the stretcher. He had a lead rope tied to the two horses and guided them over ground that was fairly level with not too many obstructions.

The gentle swaying movement of his transport brought Russell to the surface of consciousness. The first thing he sensed was the terrible numbing pain in his chest. He lay still, afraid to move in case it would exacerbate the pain.

With some effort he managed to open his eyes. The sky swayed jerkily above him. He closed his eyes again and saw violent red and white lights flashing inside his lids. The pain in his chest grew and seemed to be spreading around the rest of his body.

He remembered the wood and falling asleep. Rod Krantz and his sidekick Gill Stern had followed him. Once again he saw the gun in Rod Krantz's hand. Saw the orange flame blossom from the nozzle and felt the terrible jolt in his chest as the bullet hit him.

Uncle Clive had shown his real nature. He had sent his killers to silence his nephew. Marian Lynas had not lied. In all likelihood, Clive Dane had murdered his own brother. And now he had murdered his brother's son.

Pa, he thought, I'm on my way to join you.

Thankfully the pain lessened and faded as a terrible black hole sucked him inward and downward.

25

'What are you going to do, Clive?'

Clive Dane smiled as he replied to Gertrude's question. 'I'll go into town and see him.'

'But you can't. He's threatening to kill all the Danes that come against him.'

'He's a kid. All kids are loud-mouthed and boastful. I'll talk to him. Make him see reason.'

'Oh Clive, you don't have to go. I couldn't stand it if anything happened to you.'

Clive moved to her and put his big hands on her shoulders. 'Gertrude, I can handle myself come what may. I've been in tougher situations than this. Now don't you worry. I'll ride into town, see this fella as says he has an argument with our family and sort it out.'

'You don't realize what this is all about. This feud has been going on for years. I don't know what the cause was. Some say it was over a woman but I dismissed that. Charlie was always faithful to me. Anyway, Forten challenged Charlie and they shot it out. Forten was killed and now his son wants to carry on the vendetta. Russell had some bother with him when they were at the academy together. I think that was one of the reasons Russell was reluctant to go back there.'

'Gertrude, I'll still talk to him. Maybe we can end this feuding peaceably. I reckon it's worth a try anyhow.' He turned and walked to the door. 'Now don't fret. I'll be back for supper.'

Gertrude Dane stood, her face troubled as she watched her dead husband's brother leave. She was thinking of that dead husband and her missing son. She did not want to lose another member of the Dane family.

'Are you armed, Clive?' she suddenly called out.

He was in the act of collecting his hat. Turning to her, he placed it on his head, then with a wide grin, opened his jacket. There was no sign of any gun belt. 'I am not a violent man, Gertrude. I said I would settle this peaceably. Trust me.'

Then he was gone.

Clive Dane rode into Elsinburg alone. The Cosmopolitan was the most likely spot to find the young firebrand who had come to town and thrown out his challenge to the Dane clan. He tied up outside and then walked in to the bar-room. For a moment he stood just inside the doors and looked around the big room.

The Cosmopolitan was pretentious in its decor. Gilt mirrors lined up behind the bar. Huge round chandeliers were spaced around the room. When lit at night the place was awash with smoky radiance. During the day, light filtered through the spacious stained-glass windows.

There was no need to introduce himself. Almost as soon as he walked inside a hush fell over the saloon. Drinkers slid surreptitiously away from the long bar that ran the length of the building. Their actions isolated a group of young men. They turned and looked at the man standing inside the doorway. Cautiously, they separated, easing hands towards holstered guns.

Clive Dane strolled up to the now deserted bar. He smiled easily at the group of young men glaring at him with hostile eyes. 'Howdy, fellas.' Clive glanced around him. 'We seem to be the only ones interested in drinking. Can I buy you fellas a drink?'

One of the men detached himself slightly from his companions. 'Your name wouldn't be Dane by any chance?'

Again Clive smiled easily. 'Dane,' he said thoughtfully. 'Why would you be looking for Dane?'

'Because all Danes are cowardly dogs and I aim to shoot me a few afore I leave town.'

'You sure you won't have a drink?'

'You deaf, old man? I said I'm here to shoot me a few Danes. One especially I want to kill – name of Russell. He ran from me once. Next time we meet he won't be able to run cause he'll be dead.'

Clive Dane nodded as if in agreement with the sentiments being expressed. 'And you are. . . ?' he asked. 'I don't think we've been introduced.'

'Leonard Forten. That name should strike terror into any Dane mongrel.'

'Bottle and glasses,' Clive ordered from the scared-looking barkeep.

With trembling hands, the man set the order on the bar. As he was talking and ordering his drink Clive was moving closer and closer to Forten. As he poured his drink, only a few feet separated the protagonists.

'You sure you won't join me?'

Forten narrowed his eyes. 'Who are you?'

'Me? I'm Russell Dane's uncle.'

The boy tensed, his hand hovering over his gun butt. 'Then you're a dead Dane. Pull your iron.'

Slowly Clive Dane raised his glass and drank.. He sat the glass on the bar and turned slowly to face the angry young man. Cautiously and very slowly he gripped the edges of his jacket and raised the garment to expose his waist.

106

'I ain't carrying no irons, Lenny. Now why don't we sit and have a drink and a little parley. I have a feeling you and me have something in common. We shouldn't be quarrelling you and me. I have a proposition to offer you.'

'Toby.' Forten spoke to one of his friends standing just behind him. 'Give this cowardly old man your gun. We got nothing to talk about.'

A smirking youngster stepped up to the older man unbuckling his gun belt. As he came between Dane and Forten, that was when Clive made his move.

He reached for the belt with his right hand. At the same time he gripped the bottle he had been drinking from and swiped it across Toby's temple. As the youngster fell sideways, instead of taking the belt, Clive snatched the gun from the holster. With one swift move Clive grasped Forten by the shirt and pulled him close. At the same time he jammed the nozzle of the purloined revolver into the soft tissue underneath the youngster's chin. So fast had the rancher moved that everyone was taken by surprise. The gang of youths backing Forten were caught gaping at the sudden turn of events.

'Tell your friends to unload their weapons into the sawdust otherwise they'll have to scrape your brains off the ceiling of this here saloon.'

Forten stared venomously at his captor. There was complete silence in the saloon as everyone watched with anticipation the drama taking place at the bar.

'Do as he says.' The order was ground out through clenched teeth.

Clive never took his eyes from Forten as he listened to the muffled thud of revolvers hitting the floor. Releasing his hold on the youngster's shirt, he deftly plucked the last remaining weapon from his captive. He exchanged it for the one he had snatched from the unfortunate Toby, now standing with his friends and rubbing the bump on the side of his head.

'Now let's have that drink.'

He motioned with the revolver towards a table. As the bunch of youths moved, Clive shook his head.

'Just me and Lenny here. You fellas stay here and watch over those weapons. Make sure no one picks one up by mistake. Barkeep, I'd sure appreciate another bottle delivered to this here table. That last one went to Toby's head.'

'Yes sir, Mr Dane, sir,' the barkeep chirruped, obviously relieved the immediate threat of gunplay was averted. 'One bottle coming up, Mr Dane, sir. One bottle on the house.'

'Right, young Forten, let's you and me talk.'

26

Leonard Forten glared malevolently across the table at the man he was itching to kill. This was a member of the hated Dane clan. He felt humiliated and angry. He had boasted to his cronies he would finish this feud once and for all and kill the coward, Russell Dane, and any of his family he came across. Now at the first encounter he was forced to sit across the table from a man who claimed to be the uncle of the person Forten hated most in the world. He was helpless to do anything about it, for the insufferable Dane sat holding the youngster's own gun on him. Inwardly he was fuming as he glared his hate.

The barkeep arrived at the table with a fresh bottle of bourbon and glasses.

'Thanks,' Dane said. He indicated with the captured pistol the gang of frustrated youths standing at the bar. 'Tell them young'uns everything's on me tonight. They're to drink, carouse and whore as they will. You put it all on my tab.'

The barkeep grinned widely. 'Sure thing, Mr Dane, I'll tell them.'

With the departure of the barkeep Clive Dane leaned towards young Forten and did a surprising thing. He pushed the youngster's pistol across the table towards him. Forten looked uncertainly from the pistol to the big man sitting opposite. Clive Dane poured two drinks and pushed one glass so that it lined up beside the weapon. He raised his own drink and sipped thoughtfully.

'OK, young fella, there's your gun. If after we have finished talking you still wanna shoot then I shan't stop you.'

Forten reached out and his hand hovered above the pistol. For long stretched-out seconds he stayed like that. Slowly the tension went out of him and he picked up the glass. Beneath the table Clive Dane palmed the pocket gun that would have blown a hole in Leonard Forten had he picked up the revolver.

'What have you got to say to me, Dane? Say it quick before I change my mind and pick up that pistol.'

'Firstly, let me tell you a little about myself. For a goodly number of years I lived down in Texas. My brother Charlie and his family were as much strangers to me as were you and your family. It is only recently I have returned to this part of the world. So this feud you have with Charlie Dane and his son has completely passed me by. But I would appreciate it if you put me in the picture and tell me why you are on a killing spree targeting my nephew.'

Forten tossed down his drink and poured himself another.

'You mean you don't know what happened between my father and Charlie Dane?'

'I've only heard the Danes' version of events. You tell me how it really happened.'

Slowly, Leonard Forten leaned into the table and stared at the pistol lying so invitingly, so near his hand.

'Charlie Dane and my father had an argument. No one seems to know what it was about. There were rumours it was over a female. But no one I speak to can tell me proper. My father called Dane out. He was no gunman. For him the issue was a matter of honour. Your brother murdered my father. I aim to revenge that murder.'

It was Clive Dane's turn to reach for the bourbon and pour a drink. At the same time he topped up that of Forten.

'In that case you did right to come gunning for the Danes. Any red-blooded man would have done the same. In all respects, your version of events is roughly similar to what I heard. However I can add one little piece to the puzzle.' Beneath the table Clive Dane again slid out the pocket gun. 'Before I divulge this information let me tell you that I intensely disliked my brother Charlie and his obnoxious son, Russell. I'm glad he's dead. And the sooner his son Russell joins him the better.'

Forten frowned thoughtfully at the man opposite.

'Charlie Dane was an arrogant, despicable man,' Clive continued. 'He was a lecher who lusted after other men's women. It was his womanizing ways that led to the trouble with your father. It was this that caused his own death in the end. It was poetic justice if you ask me.'

'What do you mean?'

'You heard that Russell is on the run?'

Forten raised his eyebrows, evidently surprised at the news. 'What do you mean – on the run? I've only just arrived in Elsinburg. I ain't had time to find out anything.'

'Charlie Dane was having an affair with Marian Lynas, the wife of the local sheriff. Sheriff Lynas found out and murdered Charlie. Being sheriff, he was able to cover up his crime.'

Leonard Forten was sitting opposite, his eyes fixed on the speaker's face.

'Somehow Russell found out and tried to blackmail the sheriff. There was some shooting and the sheriff and his wife were both slain by Russell.'

'That's impossible. Russell Dane is a coward. He ran away when I challenged him to a duel.'

Clive Dane shook his head from side to side. 'That's a puzzle to me too. I guess he tricked the sheriff in some way or Lynas was trying to protect his wife and got caught out. Anyway, at the end of the night both lay dead and Russell was apprehended with their blood on his hands. The town tried to lynch him. His mother begged me to help, so I rescued him.'

'You rescued the fella as you say you dislike so much!'

'Hell, Forten, I want to marry his mother. On Charlie's death she inherited a helluva lot of land and cattle.'

'What was the piece of the puzzle you said you could provide me regarding my father's murder?'

Clive Dane was again holding the small pistol underneath the table aimed at the young man's groin.

'The woman involved in the Forten-Dane feud was . . . was your mother.'

27

'You're a liar!'

Leonard Forten kicked back his chair. It fell with a crash on to the sawdust-covered floor. The youngster was white-faced as he glared with genuine hatred at the older man still seated at the table. He slammed his hands onto the table and leaned into them. One hand was dangerously close to the revolver that Clive Dane had left so temptingly on the table.

'You're a goddamn, stinking, Dane liar.'

People in the Cosmopolitan were turning towards the confrontation. The group of youths at the bar shifted uneasily and shuffled a few steps closer to their friend. The atmosphere of impending violence was almost tangible.

Clive Dane sat easily in his chair looking relaxed. The table masked the small gun he was holding close to his thigh as he watched Forten.

'Lenny, Lenny,' he chided. 'Sit down. Everyone's looking this way. What I just revealed to you I've told no one else. There was only one man who could have told me this.' Clive Dane stared hard at the youngster standing before him, trembling with such passion and emotion. 'We have a lot in common, you and I. So before you pick up that gun and blow me to kingdom come, sit down and listen.'

Leonard Forten let his gaze slide from the hated figure sitting opposite, so cool and relaxed, and stared at the gun. His every instinct was to snatch up the weapon and kill the man opposite. Somehow the very coolness and aplomb with which his adversary sat regarding him unnerved him. He was remembering the speed and the ease with which the big man had disarmed him back at the bar. Slowly the tension went out of him. Still trembling, he sat.

'We have nothing in common, you and I, Dane. Take back what you said about my mother.'

Clive Dane sighed deeply. 'Let me tell you why I went away from here and stayed all those years in Texas. My brother Charlie and I ran the family ranch as a partnership. I was engaged to marry Gertrude Parsons. The wedding day was all set. Then one day I happened to come in from work a mite early. I found my brother in bed with my fiancée. We fought. Then I lit out for Texas. I knew if I stayed I would kill my brother for what he had done.' He paused and shook his head. 'Charlie never changed. He was a serpent that crept into other men's beds.' He looked hard at the youngster sitting opposite. 'That's what I meant when I say you and I have a lot in common. That's why your pa called out my brother. He did what any honourable man would do.'

Clive Dane sat back and watched the youngster. Most of what he had said was a fabrication. He had never been engaged to Gertrude.

'How do you know this thing?' Leonard Forten asked, his voice in a low whisper and trembling with emotion.

'Charlie told me. He boasted about it at the same time he told me about the sheriff's wife, Marian Lynas. When Lynas killed Charlie, no one was more pleased at the outcome than me.'

There was silence between the two men. Leonard Forten's head hung low as he stared unseeing at the table. Clive Dane contentedly sipped his bourbon watching the youngster. At last, Forten scrubbed a hand across his eyes. Clive Dane was sure he was wiping away tears.

'So where's Dane now?' Forten asked in a low voice.

A slow smile spread across the older man's face. 'After we pulled him out of that lynching, his mother and I thought it best if he left the area for a time. Two of my men escorted him down to Texas for his own safety. The climate where I sent him is most unhealthy. I don't expect him to survive the trip. I'm awaiting confirmation of this.'

For long moments the young man stared hard at Clive Dane. In time, he nodded. 'It figgers. You're a Dane so you're capable of such treachery. I'm still finding it hard to believe anything you tell me.' His eyes narrowed thoughtfully. 'How long ago was this?'

For the first time Clive Dane looked uncertain. 'Funny you should ask. That was a couple of months ago. I've had no word since. I've made enquiries. My contacts in Texas assure me that neither Russell nor my two men arrived there. Somewhere between here and Texas they disappeared.' He shook his head in bafflement. 'It makes me uneasy not knowing. Russell is as much a snake as was his father. It's just possible he bribed those two gunnies into betraying me. It worries me he'll turn up sometime and queer my pitch with Gertrude. She won't marry me less Russell is best man.' He eyed the youngster speculatively. 'So, when I say we have a lot in common, you can see I meant it.'

Leonard Forten scowled across at the older man. 'The only thing we have in common is the wish to see Russell Dane resting in Boot Hill.'

Clive Dane relaxed. They had passed the danger mark. For the time being, the gullible kid in front of him believed everything he had been told. His desire for revenge was turned away from himself. Clive had to utilize that vengeful craving to his own advantage. He was content to allow the youngster to stew over what he had told him. The poison bait had been laid. Patiently he waited for the lure to be taken. It did not take long. Forten leaned across the table and stared hard at the man opposite before speaking.

'So if I tell you I will not rest content till Russell Dane is dead, what would you say to that?'

Clive Dane smiled. 'Mr Forten, you would not expect me to endorse your sentiments. However, I could point you in the right direction to enable you to fulfil your ambition.'

'How so?'

'The last place they were seen was at a place called Dartsville. After that, my men and Russell seem to have vanished. Between us we may smoke him out if he's gone into hiding. I can't rest easy in my bed till I know that ghost from the past has been laid to rest.'

For a moment the two men eyed each other across the table. Clive Dane tensed as Leonard Forten reached out and picked up the revolver. He need not have worried. With a slick movement the youngster holstered his weapon. Then he picked up his drink.

'I think we have an understanding then. Let's drink to the death of Russell Dane.'

28

The youngster whose death was being discussed was sitting outside a log cabin peeling potatoes. He looked pale and thin. Weak sunlight filtered into the clearing in which the cabin was situated. The clearing was in a spruce forest. Trees grew thickly all around. To one side of the clearing, boards had been nailed to sawn-off tree stubs to form a long table. Benches made after the same fashion ran alongside the table.

The scene seemed tranquil and idyllic except for the noise coming from inside the log cabin. A raucous voice was massacring an old sea ditty.

Nassau gals ain't got no combs,
Hey-o, Suziannaahh,
They comb their hair with big whalebones,
Round the Bay of Mexico.

The singing stopped and a voice called out. 'You finished them there peelings, young Hambone?'

'Almost, Peg. Not many to go now.'

'Well, bring them in when you done. Then go fetch some more clean water from the stream.'

'If'n I never see another potato in my life, I sure as hell won't be sorry,' Russell muttered.

He surveyed the three wooden buckets he had filled with scraped potatoes. He gathered two of the buckets by their rawhide handles and carried them into the cabin.

'There you are Peg. Enough potatoes there to feed an army.'

'I am feeding an army, knucklehead – an army of vultures. I keep telling you, Hambone, you'll rue the day you made the acquaintance of these buckaroos.'

When asked his name, Russell had thought to call himself Hamlyn Danemark. The woman left off kneading dough and stood with arms akimbo as she gazed at the youth.

'Hamlyn, not Hambone,' he said, patiently.

'So you keep reminding me, Hambone, but I think Hambone suits you better.'

The woman in the cabin was very big and very round. Her

neck was non-existent and she had a round plump body on which rested her pumpkin-shaped head. Small black eyes like raisins pushed into bread dough peered out at Russell.

'How you feel now, boy? You getting better?'

'Sure, Peg. I reckon it's all that there good food you keep serving up to me as is doing it.'

The cook cackled loudly.

'Ah Hambone, you think your sweet talk'll get you extra portions of my blueberry pie. You know the rules. You don't work – you don't eat. Now go and get that water like I told you.'

Russell grinned and went back outside. As he left, the woman had returned to the dough. He heard her talking to herself as she worked the mixture.

'That Hambone, he sure one sweet talker. I'm sure he try sweet talk me into giving him extra pie.'

This latter was followed by a giggle then the big woman launched into the chorus of her song. Russell grimaced and, grabbing up two empty buckets, walked into the trees to fetch water.

For all her nagging at him, he owed much of his recovery from the bullet wound in his chest to the loving care the woman had lavished on him.

This is where the outlaws had brought him after they had rescued him. This was their eating-place. The outlaws lived separate in a cave further up the valley. During his weeks of recovery, Russell had gradually learned the big woman's history and why she had chosen to bury herself in this remote place to cook for a bunch of outlaws.

Peg had run a high-class whorehouse in Denver. The story went, as told to him by Myron Holly, that Peg had badly injured a young man one night in the brothel. He had been beating up a young prostitute when Peg intervened. In the

117

ensuing fracas the big woman hit the youngster. In falling, he banged his head. He never recovered from the injury.

'The boy was an idiot ever since. Had to be cared for day and night. Couldn't feed himself – couldn't clean himself.'

'But why did she run? Surely it was accidental?' Russell asked.

'In ordinary circumstances that plea might have worked to get her off. However the fella as was injured was the son of a judge. He controlled the court and she was sentenced to hang. Peg broke out of jail and went on the run. She knows while she stays here she's safe. The arrangement works to our advantage. If Peg weren't here cooking for us we'd all as likely as not be dead of indigestion. Afore she arrived we had burnt beans for breakfast, burnt beans for dinner and burnt beans for supper. The coffee was hogwash and the bread and biscuits set to ruin a man's teeth.'

Russell grinned at the picture painted of the pre-Peg outlaws' diet.

'Now she's got her own pet potato peeler and washer boy, she's never been happier.'

That had wiped the smile from Russell's face.

'Consarn it, Myron, can't I come over and stay with you boys?'

'Nope, Peg says no. And when Peg makes up her mind about something, you can bet us hard-bitten, ornery outlaws take notice.'

But Russell was making progress and gaining in strength every day. The bullet in his chest still lay there. No one in the outlaw camp had wanted to take the responsibility for digging it out. The pain had all but disappeared. He was strong but he knew he needed to be stronger. There were other things he needed to be working on. He decided to tackle this at supper.

Platters of steaming potatoes sat on the boards along-side slabs of roast. Jugs of home-brewed corn beer were spaced at intervals along with water and fresh milk. Eager outlaws sat at the makeshift table staring hungrily at the food piled on the table. They knew better than to start before Peg said grace.

'Gawd amighty, in your heaven above, look down on these starving heathens and make them grateful for your bountiful mercy.'

A chorus of 'Amens' rang out and the men immediately fell too, spearing the food and heaping their plates with the hot grub.

Russell had managed to seat himself beside Myron Holly. He waited till Myron was chewing contentedly before he initiated the conversation.

'Myron, I need a favour from you.'

'What's that, Hambone? What sorta favour?'

Peg's nickname had taken favour amongst the outlaws. It had more potency as the youngster had protested against the corruption of his false name.

'I need my gun back.'

Myron went on eating as he thought about this.

'Why?'

'I never told you why those two fellas shot me.'

Myron made no answer to this observation.

'They were paid to kill me.'

Myron nodded. 'Yeah, I know that. They told Elias as much afore they tried to kill him.'

'I gotta go back and face the man as paid them killers. I need my gun to practice.'

The outlaw finally turned and stared at the youngster looking so earnestly back at him. 'This man as paid to have you killed – he wealthy?'

'I guess. He's probably married my mother by now and taken over my father's ranch. It's a big spread – thousands of acres.'

Myron frowned. 'Why'd he want you dead?'

'He killed my pa. I found out and now he wants me silenced.'

'If he's as wealthy as you say, he'll hire more men to kill you.'

'I ain't hiding all my life from him.'

'You handy with a Colt then?'

Russell shrugged. 'Not particular, that's why I wanna practice. I want you to teach me.'

'Goddamn, I missed my extra portion of potatoes,' Myron complained, looking at the empty platters. 'Son, just let this matter drop till we finish eating.'

'I gotta know. I need that goddamn gun,' Russell muttered under his breath.

Myron glared balefully at the youngster. 'Shaddup!' he suddenly yelled.

Russell subsided sulkily.

Pie was served up accompanied by jugs of molasses. There were groans of appreciation all around the table. Russell lifted his spoon. Before he could dig it into the pastry, a hand reached over and took the dish away. He glared angrily at a grinning Myron.

'Tell you what, kid. Let's strike a bargain. You give me your portion of pie and I teach you to shoot.'

For a moment Russell stared in surprise at the outlaw. 'If that's what it takes, then I agree.' Suddenly a thought struck him. 'How do I know if you're any good?'

Myron eyed the youngster shrewdly. 'You've already asked the boys about me, ain't you?'

Russell had the grace to blush. 'They said as no one was

120

faster than you with a gun.'

'Then every night you want a lesson you hand me your pie.'

'You drive a hard bargain, Myron Holly, but I agree.'

29

'Hambone, there ain't no more I can teach you.'

Myron Holly was ejecting spent shells from his Colt as he spoke. Beside him, Russell was performing the same task.

Every afternoon the outlaw had led Russell into the woods where they had practiced the craft of the fast draw. Russell had his own gun rig that Holly had found in the outlaw's den and handed over to the youngster.

'Am I fast, Myron?'

For a moment, the outlaw regarded the youngster. He was contrasting the corpse-like figure they had carried into the camp some months back. No one had expected the kid to survive, but Peg had taken him under her wing and nursed him back from the brink of the grave. Colour had crept back into the youngster's face and he was putting on weight.

'Yeah, son, you're fast all right. But it's one thing firing at targets painted on tree trunks and it's another matter altogether shooting at a man what's shooting back. If you flinch or cringe away then you're dead.'

Russell did not look up at the outlaw but stared down at the carpet of pine needles in the little clearing where they came to practice every day.

'I ran away from a challenge once. Since that time I tried to convince myself it was because I received a telegram telling me my father was dead. Sometimes I almost believe it was true and at times I fear I am a coward.'

'Hambone, I've taught you all I know. At first I was reluctant to pass on my gun-fighting skills to a youngster. Maybe if 'n I didn't have this ability with a gun I wouldn't be here skulking in hiding with a miserable bunch of outlaws. I could'a been herding cows or even have my own little homestead somewheres. But that was my choice and I'm stuck with it. I guess you gotta go back and brace the fella as sicked those gunnies on to you.'

'Thanks, Myron, whatever happens I'll never forget you.'

'Hell, I'm gonna miss those extra helpings of blueberry pie.'

Holly turned and walked away. Russell watched him for a while then turned and stared at the bullet-scarred trees against which he had honed his skills with his Colt .44. He felt a shiver of apprehension as he contemplated what he had to do.

'Goddamn it, Clive killed Pa and then hired Gill Stern and Rod Krantz to gun me down.'

He remembered the terror he felt as Rod Krantz had pointed the Colt. There had been that terrible blow on his chest and the pain and darkness that followed. He drew a shuddering breath, then turned and headed back towards the cabin.

It would be an awful lot easier to stay here with the outlaw gang. He was outside the law himself and was wanted for the slaying of Sheriff Lynas. Surely, when he turned up in Elsinburg, he would be arrested and thrown in jail once more. Again he shivered as he recalled the bestial faces of the men that gathered to lynch him.

He had encountered those same men on numberless occasions in the day-to-day life of the town. In the streets

122

and in the stores they had greeted him as a familiar friend and neighbour. He had seen them imbibing liquor in the Cosmopolitan Saloon. On that terrible day they had turned from ordinary decent citizens into crazy men. Faces contorted by hate, they had howled like bloodthirsty beasts for his life. Could he face that threat again?

Then there was Uncle Clive. In some ways he was more dangerous than the mob. How could he face up to a man that could murder his own brother and send paid killers to slay his nephew?

'Like a rattlesnake without the warning rattles,' he muttered, and wondered how his mother would take the scandal of her brother-in-law's perfidy.

'Even if she's married to Clive already, I still gotta do it.'

The more he thought over his options, the more confused and uneasy he became. By suppertime he had still not made up his mind to leave the outlaw's hideout. Over the meal he was moody and thoughtful.

'Consarn it, Hambone, you look as if your guts have gone all sour on you. You have a face on you like a coyote's backside,' Elias Carter complained at last, plainly irked by the youngster's moody silence.

Russell stared at the outlaw chief and it was as if the decision had been made for him. 'I been thinking over what I ougthta do, Elias. It's time I went home.'

The outlaw chief eyed Russell thoughtfully. 'You ain't going anywhere, kid.'

Russell frowned. 'What do you mean?'

Elias Carter smiled easily. 'This is your home. When we brung you here it was on the understanding that you were one of us – an outlaw. You understand what that means. You think we gonna let you ride outta here knowing where our hideout is an' all?'

Russell stared at the outlaw, puzzled by his comment. 'How do you mean? What difference does that make?'

'Do I hav'ta spell it out for you? You're part of the gang now. I can't let you ride outta here and risk you bringing back a posse.' Carter shook his head. 'Nosiree, once in, never out.'

'Goddamn it, I ain't bringing no posse back here. You fellas saved my life. What sorta lowlife you take me for!'

'Yeah? And what happens when they put that noose around your neck and you're fearing for your life? You'll begin to think there's maybe one way to save your neck being stretched.' In a falsetto voice the outlaw chief continued. 'Oh dear citizens, don't hang me. I know where you can bring in a whole passel of baddies. I'll take you to them and you can hang a dozen of them there outlaws instead of just one little old me.'

There was silence around the table and the men had stopped eating. They watched the kid as he sat taut-faced, glaring at the chief. Suddenly, Russell was on his feet. His hand hovered over the pistol he had been firing at trees.

'I'm leaving here. There's a job I have to do.' Russell's voice was tight with nervousness as he spoke. 'Don't no one try to stop me.'

Elias Carter laughed then. 'What kid – you gonna take us all on?'

'I don't wanna fight with the men as saved my life, but I gotta go back to Elsinburg and face up to the man as murdered my pa and tried to kill me.'

Carter stood up from the table. He was smiling cynically at the youngster all keyed up before him.

'Let's see just how well Myron has taught you. You ready to use that iron?'

There was a scramble from around the table as men got

out of the firing line. Russell's insides began to quiver as he realized the position the outlaw chief had placed him in. Elias Carter waited for the youngster to make his play.

'Hurry up, kid, my supper's getting cold,' the bandit taunted. 'That Colt you wearing just an ornament or are you gonna use it?'

30

The moments stretched out interminably. Sweat began to form on Russell's brow. He stared at the bandit leader.

Watch his eyes, Myron had instructed, *you'll see his eyes change. It ain't much – just a subtle shift and then you know he's going to make his move.*

Elias Carter's eyes gave nothing away. He stared cold and unmoving at Russell. And suddenly the agitation and tension that Russell felt went.

A great calm settled on him. Confidence swelled and eddied through him. Afterwards, he wondered if this change was reflected in his eyes, for at that precise moment Elias Carter's hand dipped for his gun. Hardly knowing how it got there, Russell's Colt was in his hand. Flame belched from the outlaw's gun at the same time his own gun was bucking in his hand. Something hit Russell and he was flung sideways even as he was triggering his shot.

He was on the ground with a pair of brawny arms wrapped round him.

'Goddamn it, let me go!' Russell fumed.

'Not till you see sense, you dumb kid.' It was Peg's voice in his ear. 'You wanna get yourself killed! Now stop struggling and promise me you'll put that iron away if'n I let you up.'

'Let me go! It's what I gotta do!'

Myron Holly resolved the dilemma for them both.

'Let him up, Peg,' he called. 'It's over.'

Russell sagged, all the tension suddenly draining out of him. 'All right then, lemme go, I won't start anything.'

Slowly the pair disentangled. Still holding his weapon, Russell scrambled to his feet and looked up at the supper table. He blinked in surprise. A form was slumped across the table, the hand still grasping the Colt. Blood seeped onto the boards of the trestle table and dripped steadily to the ground. Elias Carter had fought his last gunfight and lost out against a green kid.

'Goddamn kid shot Elias!' one of the bandits yelled.

'Get the murdering sumbitch!'

Russell was still holding his Colt. Suddenly alert to the danger from the rest of the gang, he brought up the gun to cover the men gathered around the table.

'I . . . I never wanted this. He forced me into it. Don't make me kill again.'

'You gonna take us all on, kid?' The squint-eyed Ichabod Goodyear was leering across at Russell. 'There's a dozen of us an' only one of you.'

Russell stared back, his eyes steady as he took in the members of the gang gathered round the table.

'I'll shoot anyone as tries to stop me. All I ever wanted was to ride back to Elsinburg and square things with the men as tried to kill me. There's a good chance I'll be shot or hanged back there. It don't mean nothing to me if I have to shoot a few of you to get there or if I get shot as well. I might as well die here as back in Elsinburg. But I will take some of you with me.'

Russell watched the men as they weighed up his words. He had just shot Elias Carter and his gun was still in his hand. That gun was pointing at the bandits but more especially it was aimed squarely at Ichabod Goodyear. The mean-faced Goodyear licked his lips.

'Don't let him fool you – he's only a kid,' Goodyear snarled. 'That was a fluke shot. The kid pulled first afore Elias had a chance. Get the sumbitch.'

The men shifted uneasily. Russell could see they were undecided. Some had their hands on gun butts, but no one wanted to chance beating the Colt that Russell was already pointing at them.

'That's enough!'

The voice cut across the tension. Everyone turned to look at the man who spoke. Myron Holly strolled forward. His thumbs were hooked casually in his gun belt.

'You all saw what happened. Elias drew first. Hambone was faster. I guess I taught him better than I thought. The kid wants to leave. I say let him go.'

'You heard what Elias said,' Ichabod Goodyear said in his thin mean voice. 'He'll bring back a posse.'

'That's nonsense and you all know it. When we brung Hambone in he was near dead. He has no idea where we're located. I say we blindfold him and take him out a'ways and let him go.'

There were murmurs of agreement from amongst the outlaws.

'I say Myron's right. It was a fair fight.'

'Hey, Hambone, you could take Carter's place. Seeing as you killed him an' we got to elect us a new leader.'

That brought a chorus of guffaws. Suddenly the tension dissipated.

'Dang me, I ain't finished my supper,' someone remarked.

Suddenly the men were drifting back to the table.

Without ceremony the dead body of Elias Carter was pulled from the table and dragged to one side. Peg came up and threw a towel across the blood that stained the table.

'I'll bring fresh coffee,' she offered.

Russell sat down at the table and, picking up a biscuit, chewed morosely. He had a feeling of light-headedness and emptiness. Around him the men were excitedly discussing the shooting. Peg arrived with the pot of steaming coffee. She filled Russell's mug and moved on to the head of the table. Before the cook reached her seat there was a sudden hush. Russell looked up. The men were staring not at him but at Ichabod Goodyear.

He looked across the table at the mean-spirited bandit. Goodyear had his pistol out and was resting the butt on the table and was it was pointing straight at Russell.

'I figure I'm taking over this gang. The first thing I'm gonna do is kill this sumbitch as killed Elias.'

Once more the tension was heavy in the air as the men sat motionless, waiting for Ichabod Goodyear to carry out his threat. Russell stared at the nozzle of the gun pointed across the table at him. He had a sudden vision of Rod Krantz's face leering at him from behind his Colt. The flash and the bang were still very vivid in his mind. He had survived that. He had outgunned Elias Carter. A fatalistic calm settled on him.

'Think you can beat this bullet, Hambone?' Ichabod Goodyear asked, leering at Russell.

The youngster stared steadily into the bandit's eyes. He was at a disadvantage sitting down. His gun was in the holster. He knew what had to be done. He would throw himself backwards off the bench and try for his gun at the same time.

'Go to hell, Ichabod!' Russell said, and everything

happened at once.

Peg threw the coffee pot and it hit Ichabod Goodyear in the side of the head. Hot liquid spilled down on to his gun hand. Goodyear yelled and his Colt went off. Russell was falling backwards and pulling his Colt at the same time. He fired under the table at Goodyear. He pumped three shots at the target. The man was screaming and trying to stand up. His Colt had fallen to the table. Still screaming, he fell back out of his seat and onto the ground. He rolled about in agony, holding his hands to his groin. Russell lay on his back and cursed long and hard.

31

'You sure you don't wanna take over this here gang of outlaws?'

Myron Holly, Peg and Russell were sitting in Peg's cabin drinking coffee. Russell stared in bewilderment at Myron.

'Hell, Myron, are you joshing me or what?'

Myron pursed his lips and looked over at his protégé. 'You could do worse. After all, you just killed two top men in the gang. You're the logical choice to lead these fellas. Just think on it. There you are, not turned twenty an' you got yourself a readymade gang of cut-throats. The dime novels will love it.'

'I ain't cut out to be no gang boss. If anyone should take over it should be you, Myron. And, anyway, I ain't never killed two men in the gang. I might have killed Elias Carter but I only wounded Ichabod Goodyear.'

'Ichabod Goodyear won't last the night. You shot his

balls off and put two slugs in his guts. Hell, Hambone, I done gone and trained me a goddamn killin' machine.'

Myron Holly shook his head in wonderment.

'Don't fret none, Myron. That's why I'm in this mess in the first place. You didn't set me on the downward path. I killed myself a sheriff afore I met you. Anyways, I wish you all would stop calling me Hambone. My given name is Russell.'

Peg and Myron looked at each other and began to grin. Russell sighed.

'You saved my life out there, Peg. I guess you can call me what you like.'

'Humph,' sniffed Peg. 'I done gone an' nursed you back from the edge of death. You think I gonna let that low down Ichabod Goodyear undo all that good work. I thought I was saving you afore when Elias braced you. I see now you already had his measure. You had him killed afore I could pull you off'n him.'

'I reckon that's one killing I do regret. Elias saved my life when he brung me back here and handed me over to you.' Russell shook his head in bewilderment. 'Why he wanna pull a stunt like that beats me.' He sighed deeply and stared morosely into his coffee mug. 'The thing is, I must get going soonest. Myron, I don't mind if'n you wanna do what you said and blindfold me afore leaving here.' He grinned ruefully. 'I'll probably get lost anyways. I was lost afore Rod Krantz and Gill Stern found me.'

'Hell, kid, I been thinking things over. I'm athinking I will lead you outta here and then I've a mind to tag along with you. I'm getting tired of this here outlaw life. I'll escort you back to Elsinburg and then mosey on west. They say as there's gold been found in the Black Hills. I guess I could lose myself in them there gold diggin's. Who's to know, I might even strike it rich.'

'Myron, now you got me to thinking,' interjected Peg. 'Would you take a travelling companion with you? Maybe I could open a restaurant for hungry miners. They say as miners'll pay a fortune for a slice of home baking. What you say about losing yourself in the diggings applies to me too. I guess Dakota's far enough away for no one to be looking too hard for an ex-whorehouse madam. Especially if'n she's running a successful eating-house.'

Russell was staring in some bewilderment at his companions. 'You fellas serious about leaving and quitting the outlaw life?'

'Sure thing, Hambone. The more I think on it, the more it appeals to me. It's a long trek to Dakota but if Peg comes along then her cooking will shorten the journey a mite.'

'Well I sure would welcome some company on the trip back to Elsinburg. The thing is, I got no money. I had a belt stuffed full but I guess Elias took that as payment for rescuing me.'

Myron narrowed his eyes as he stared at Russell. 'Well, I'll be. Is that what that was? I saw old Elias had that belt strapped round him. Never told no one about it nor what it was. He's laying out there in the woods ready for burial. Peg, can I take one of them lamps and go look-see.'

When he returned from his ghoulish task, Myron tossed the canvas money belt on the table in front of Russell.

'There you go, kid, still plenty in there.'

Peg reached out and stroked the belt. 'So that's where he was getting his money from. He was coming down to me for his pleasuring, morning noon and night. I wondered how he came into so much wealth. Well I'll be darned!'

'I guess we can split this three ways,' Russell said, trying not to smile at the thought of Elias Carter and Peg together. He knew most of the outlaws bartered with Peg for sexual favours.

'Hambone, that sure is mighty generous of you.' Myron said ruefully. 'I hardly got a nickel myself. Outlawing don't pay all that good. What little I did get I spent on women and whiskey and gambling.'

Russell pushed the belt towards the overweight cook. 'Peg, you take charge of that. Cut it three ways. Myron, when do you think we oughta start?'

'First thing in the morning. We'll start out like we agreed. I blindfold you and lead you outta here. Peg'll come along with her wagon as if she's going for supplies like she does. We'll be long gone afore these fellas realize we ain't coming back.'

'I guess.' Russell sighed despondently. 'I know I gotta go back to Elsinburg. It scares me some to think on it.' When he looked up at his companions they could see the anguish plain in his face. 'My uncle may already be married to my mother. Somehow I gotta tell her what sorta snake he is.' He shook his head and stared down at the table. 'I gotta go back. They might hang me – they might shoot me or they might do both but my father's murderer must be brought to justice. Whatever way the dime falls, it'll break Mother's heart.'

32

The town hadn't changed since he had left in such a hurry with a lynch mob on his tail. He sat his horse and studied the place from the road above the town.

'There she is,' Russell said to Myron Holly as he drew up beside him. 'Elsinburg – sad and corrupt. I wish I didn't have to go down there but . . .' He left the rest of his sentiments unvoiced. 'I guess this is where we part company.'

Wagon wheels rumbled up the road and Russell turned and watched Peg pull up behind them.

'I wanna thank you and Peg for all the help you gave me. I don't suppose I'll ever be able to repay you both.'

'Hambone, you'll repay us by just staying alive.'

Russell sighed heavily. 'That remains to be seen. I guess this is goodbye.'

'Not quite yet, old buddy,' Myron replied. 'After all this travelling, a fella is entitled to a drink.' He turned in the saddle and addressed his next remark to Peg. 'What about you, Peg? You feel like stopping in this here Elsinburg for a drink.'

'As long as you're gonna treat me to a decent meal along with that drink. A gal gets tired of her own cooking now an' again.'

Myron grinned. 'You got yourself a deal, Peg. You buy the drinks and I'll buy the meal.'

'Men,' grumbled Peg. 'One day I'll meet myself a real gent what'll treat me proper. Come on.'

'Hang on there, you two, when I ride down there there's apt to be trouble. We'll ride in separate.'

'Hambone,' Peg asserted. 'I didn't bring you back from the dead just to let you ride into that there hellhole on your lonesome. I'm coming in there with you.'

She flicked the reins and the wagon lumbered forward. Slowly the three travelling companions headed down the road to the town. Two of them were filled with curiosity – anxious to explore the pleasures of this new town. The third traveller was filled with deep apprehension.

Before she tied up the wagon, Peg strapped a sixgun around her ample waist. She grinned at Russell as she did so.

'Anyone as wants to lynch you'll hav'ta walk through me first.'

'Goddamn it, Peg, you don't hav'ta to do this,' Russell muttered.

For answer she slapped him on the shoulder with enough force to make him wince. 'Come on. You're just trying to get outta buying me that drink.'

The Cosmopolitan certainly hadn't changed since Russell's last visit. Drinking and gambling were going on just as the youngster remembered. The patrons took no notice of the trio that entered. They stood for a moment studying the interior of the saloon then sauntered up to the bar.

'Whiskey with three glasses, and leave the bottle.'

As he raised his drink to his lips Russell caught sight of his reflection in the gilt framed mirrors behind the bar. His lower face was covered in light, blonde stubble. A crease had appeared between his deep-set eyes. He had ridden from this town as a boy but had returned a man. He threw back his drink and reached for the bottle. Then he noticed the atmosphere in the saloon was subtly changing. The noise and chatter of men and women at play was slowly subsiding. Again he looked into the mirror only this time he was seeking the source of the change. He had not long to wait.

'It's Dane, he's come back.'

Men were staring at the youngster by the bar. For the present they had not registered his companions. Slowly Russell turned and faced the room. He stayed silent, waiting for the next move.

'Someone fetch the marshal.'

'He's on his way. The murderer was spotted coming into town.'

'We hanged you once, Dane, we'll hang you again. Only this time we'll finish the job.'

There were angry mutterings and some men stood as if intent to carry out the threat.

'Any man as wants to come up and try anything is welcome. Only this time I'm fighting back. I admit I killed Sheriff Lynas because he tried to kill me. He didn't want me blabbing out he was involved in the murder of my father. I'm willing to face a coroner's court what's legal and don't take place in Elsinburg.

'I have sour memories of this goddamn, stinking town. You're not men – just a bunch of yellow-bellies. You took an unarmed kid from an unlawful court and tried to lynch him. When my uncle rode into town and fired a few shots in the air you ran like terrified chickens. You think I'm scared of a few lousy drunks? Anyone want to try anything, now's the time.'

Russell stepped away from the bar and away from his friends. They stayed where they were but both Peg and Myron slid their hands onto their holstered guns. The angry mutterings from the crowd grew in volume.

'Goddamn fool kid.' Myron muttered so low only Peg and Russell could make out what he said. 'He's liable to get us killed afore we get to the Black Hills.'

Russell moved further away from his friends.

'Ain't no danger from these yellow-livered chickens. There ain't a man among them.'

Russell was angry. These were the same men who bayed for his blood when they dragged him from this very same saloon. He cast his scornful gaze around the crowd of men in the bar. Then he stepped closer to them. He could see some edging back.

'You!' he suddenly barked at a big, bearded man. 'You wanna try your luck?' He spread his arms wide, well away from his sides and his holstered Colt. 'I'll give you a fair chance – more'n you gave me last time. Look. I'll let you get your pistol out afore I go for my iron.'

The man nervously licked his lips, beads of sweat breaking out on his brow. He dropped his eyes and stared down at his drink. There was silence in the room. Russell felt a sense of power as he gazed round at the cowed gathering. No one moved as he swept his gaze around.

'Damned yellow-bellies,' he muttered, and contemptuously turned his back on the crowded bar.

A gun roared somewhere to his left. The bullet ploughed into the floor beside Russell. He jumped at the total unexpectedness of the shot. His hand was reaching for his own gun when the voice barked out.

'Touch that iron and the next one's in your head.'

Russell went very still.

In the doorway, a figure was silhouetted against the daylight flooding in from the street. Russell couldn't make out details, but there was no mistaking the Colt held steady in the man's hand.

33

'Russell Dane, I'm arresting you on suspicion of the murder of Sheriff Lynas and his wife. You can come quiet or be carried down to the morgue. It don't matter to me how you play it. Just now I hold the winning hand.'

For a wild moment Russell contemplated his chances of drawing and beating the gun in the doorway. It was as if the man holding the gun was reading his mind.

'I know what you're thinking. Can I get my Colt out afore he blows a hole in me? Judge Colt don't take no pris-

oners, Dane. A properly constituted court does. You make
your choice.'

Russell's shoulders slumped.

'Just walk over here, nice and peaceable like.'

A chair scraped somewhere in the body of the saloon.

'Well done, Marshal. Just leave him with us. We'll save
you the bother of a court.'

Again a shot blasted into the room.

'I'll shoot any man that moves from this saloon before
my prisoner and myself are safely down in the jail. There'll
be no more lynching. I'm the law in this town and don't
you forget it. I'll arrest any man that tries to take the law
in his own hands.'

Then the doorway was empty as the lawman and his
prisoner disappeared into the street.

The saloon erupted into a hubbub of noise as the
patrons, freed from their constraints, excitedly began talking. There was a concerted rush for the bar as men pushed
to refresh their drinks. No one took any notice of the fat
woman and her companion as they drifted to the door
and exited.

'Hell's bells, what we gonna do now?'

'That Hambone, he weren't fooling when he called this
town a hellhole. He ain't been back five minutes afore he's
arrested and slung in the can.'

Myron Holly stroked his chin thoughtfully. 'I'm thinking nobody here knows you an' me. What say we mosey on
down the jail and bust young Hambone loose.'

'You crazy, we'd have the whole town about our necks.
There wouldn't be just one lynching but three.' Peg
fingered her throat as she spoke. 'I don't think no rope
collar'd suit my delicate constitution.'

'Look, Peg, we owe it to the kid to help him out. All we

137

hav'ta do is ride up to the marshal's office an' tell him we just arrived in town looking for work. Then as his guard is down I pull my gun on him an' we spring Hambone.'

Peg made a wry face. 'What the hell! I guess we're both wanted by the law, anyways. One more crime won't make no difference.'

Myron swung onto his horse and took up the reins of Russell's mount. Peg clambered into the driving seat of her wagon and followed.

'You go in first, Peg. The marshal won't be too suspicious of a female as he would a strange gunman walking into his office.'

Peg gave him one last look and cast her eyes to the sky before pushing inside the door of the marshal's office. Myron Holly looked around to see if he was observed. The citizens of Elsinburg obviously took the marshal seriously when he told them not to follow him into the street. Taking a deep breath, Myron took out his gun and stepped inside the building.

'Nobody move,' he said harshly.

The rider pulled up outside the Dane ranch and, jumping down from his horse, ran up the steps to the front door.

'Mr Dane, he's back. Mr Dane – Russell's back in Elsinburg.'

The door was jerked open. Gertrude Dane was staring out in some bewilderment at the cowboy who had been banging on the door and yelling out his news.

'Begging your pardon, ma'am.'

'My Russell is back, you said. Oh, this is wonderful news. Is he all right? Did you talk to him?'

'No, ma'am. The marshal arrested him afore anyone gotta chance to talk to him.'

Gertrude's hand flew to her mouth. 'Arrested! Oh, it's started all over again.' She took in the dusty condition of the cowboy. 'You rode out here in a hurry to bring us the news. Mr Dane is over in Waddling selling some steers. If you took a fresh mount would you be prepared to ride over there to let him know? Clive will know what to do.'

'Sure thing, Mrs Dane. I'll start straight away.

'And tell someone to harness up my buggy. I'm leaving straightaway for town.'

Clive Dane strode into Waddling's one and only saloon, feeling very contented with life. He patted the bulge of notes he had tucked into an inside pocket. It was the proceeds from the sale of a herd he had driven over from the Dane ranch. He had insisted on cash for the transaction. Cash was not easy to trace. Clive Dane was putting by a nest egg in case his plan to marry Gertrude was delayed by any unforeseen event. The disappearance of Russell along with Gill Stem and Rod Krantz left him with an uneasy feeling. Until he was sure Russell was dead, then he was taking nothing for granted.

'Bourbon,' he ordered.

The batwing doors opened. Most men looked at the newcomer. Clive was so immersed in his daydreams he took no notice till the man arrived at the bar beside him. He recognized the cowboy as one he had recruited from his old haunts back in Texas. Over a period of time he had been getting rid of hands loyal to the former owner of the ranch and replacing them with his own recruits.

'Alex?' As he greeted the man a sense of foreboding was edging out the former feeling of well-being.

'That kid you been enquiring about – your nephew – well, he's turned up.'

The ominous presentiment in Clive Dane increased. He tried to remain calm as he faced the cowboy. 'Can I buy you a drink?'

Alex nodded and wiped his mouth. 'Sure could do with one. Thirsty work all this riding.'

'Two beers,' Clive ordered. 'Now, tell me everything.'

'The kid rode into town and braced the crowd in the Cosmopolitan. Afore they could do anything the marshal arrived and arrested him. I rode hell for leather to the ranch to tell you. Mrs Dane told me to ride over here and find you. She's gone on into Elsinburg.'

'You say the marshal arrested him. He in the jail now?'

The beers arrived and the cowboy took a long draught before replying. 'Far as I know, he's safely penned in the lockup.'

Clive Dane held his beer without drinking and stared thoughtfully into the distance. Finally he put down the beer, untouched.

'Wait here for me, Alex. I'm going down to the telegraph office. Then we'll ride back to the ranch together.'

34

Myron Holly kept his gun raised as he shouted his warning. The marshal was sitting at his desk. He looked up with some alarm at the abrupt interruption. As soon as Myron had made his dramatic entrance, Peg had pulled her gun and was pointing it at the lawman. Sitting in a chair, looking somewhat bemused, was the youth they had come to rescue.

'Hambone, take the marshal's gun. We'll lock him in

his own cage and then we'll be on our way.'

The marshal looked quizzically at his prisoner. 'Hambone? I take it these are friends of yours?'

The lawman was a heavily built young man with wide-set eyes and a broad, handsome face.

'Yeah, I'm afraid so. Horace, let me introduce Myron and Peg, my owl-hoot companions.'

'Hell, it ain't time for polite introductions, Hambone. Grab his gun,' snarled Myron. 'You.' He indicated the marshal. 'Stand up real slow and walk back to them there cells. And don't make any false moves or the citizens of this goddamn town'll be havin' to elect a new marshal.'

Russell rose from his seat and stepped up to Myron. 'Myron, it's OK. This is Marshal Horace Winterman, an old friend of mine. He's trying to help.'

Myron gaped at the lawman. 'You friendly with a goddamn lawman! What's the matter with you, Hambone? The citizens of this godforsaken town are windin' themselves up to a lynchin' and you sit there jawin' with a goddamn lawman as will help them string you up.'

'Calm down, Myron, and listen to what he has to say afore you condemn him.'

Myron looked from his Colt to Peg and then back to the marshal. 'Peg, is this really happenin'?'

Slowly Peg lowered her weapon. 'I guess we hav'ta listen to what he has to say.'

Myron sighed and looked towards the marshal. He didn't put up his Colt. 'Well?'

'Russell is an old friend of mine. When the sheriff was killed I was sent down to take over till a new sheriff was elected. I've been poking around Elsinburg trying to make sense of it all. Some details are beginning to fall into place now that I have heard Russell's side of things. The piece about his uncle being involved in the murder of his father makes sense now. I was puzzled by a bunch of messages I found in this office. They were correspondences back and forth to Texas enquiring about Russell's uncle, Clive. Obviously Sheriff Lynas wanted some background on Clive. It turns out the man has a shady background, or at least a bloody and murky past. I was just about to tell Russell all this when you fellas barged in.' The marshal paused and looked pointedly at the gun in Myron's hand. 'I'd be much obliged if 'n you would either point that there gun somewhere else or put it up.'

Myron glanced down at his Colt and then looked up at Russell. The youngster nodded.

'Myron, do as he says. Horace is on our side.'

Reluctantly Myron holstered his weapon. Peg followed suit.

'Now we got that outta the way, Hambone, shall I carry on?' the marshal asked, turning back to Russell.

The youngster groaned. 'Not you too. It looks as if I'm stuck with that name.'

'Hambone,' mused Horace. 'It kinda suits you.'

'Horace, just stick to the business in hand. You were about to tell me about my uncle Clive's shady past.'

'It appears your uncle was a hired gun. Not only did he hire his own gun but he was ramrod to a bunch of killers. You needed a killing done and could pay enough, he found the men for the job.'

'Rod Krantz and Gill Stern.' Russell was staring at the marshal. 'I never thought much of it at the time but these Texans drifted on to the ranch and Clive took them on the payroll.'

'What about this Rod Krantz and Gill Stern?'

'After Clive rescued me from the lynching he sent me out with those two Texans to keep me safe. Their job was to see I never returned.'

'What happened?'

'Rod Krantz and Gill Stern are dead,' Russell replied bleakly.

Horace sighed deeply. 'Hambone, this all fits in with your story of Clive Dane being responsible for the murder of your father. And if, as you say, Sheriff Lynas was involved in the killing or the cover-up, it makes sense for the sheriff and Clive to want you shut up. That meeting with his wife was so as he could kill you and silence you for good. It all begins to make sense.'

'Why don't you go out to the ranch and arrest him?'

'Hambone, we need proof. I could arrest him, but I doubt if I could secure a conviction. It would be your word against his. And don't forget this killing of the sheriff and his wife hangs over you. As far as the law's concerned, you're wanted for murder. How you think a jury is gonna feel about taking the word of a double murderer? Especially as it was a lawman as was killed and his wife to boot. Afore the trial was over the hangman would be getting his rope ready for your neck.

'Anyway, we can't stay here tonight if the townsfolk get wound up. That was a fool play to confront them at the Cosmopolitan. They won't like being made to eat dirt like that. My guess is, as the drink flows then they'll want to finish what they started a while back and lynch you.'

'What you suggest?'

'I been staying down at the sheriff's old house. I suggest you all go down there for now.' Horace looked over at Peg. 'Was that a wagon you pulled up in?'

'Yup. It got all my worldly goods in there. I was on my way to the gold diggings to open an eating-house.'

'Hambone, you jump in the back of that wagon so as no

one sees you and take these two down to the old Lynas house. I'll join you as soon as it is safe to do so.

'Myron, take a look out and see if there's anyone about. Then all three get the hell outta my sight. I gotta figure out how to stop this town boiling over and going on a lynching spree.'

35

Clive Dane waited at the stage depot. There were four hard-looking gunmen with him. They lounged against the wood-framed building and waited with their boss.

Their presence made the depot manager nervous. He was not used to so many dangerous-looking men hanging around at his depot, and he feared the worst. For the life of him he could not imagine what they were waiting for. He racked his brains in an attempt to figure out what had attracted the men.

Had someone sent money down with the stage and not informed him? He feared for whatever booty the stage was carrying and he feared for his job. If the stage company could not trust him with the news of a valuable consignment they perhaps meant to replace him with someone they could trust. As he worried over these things, he nervously pulled out his timepiece and consulted it every minute or so.

Only one of the men was vaguely familiar to him and that was the man Dane. What would a respectable rancher be doing hanging round with a bunch of hard cases? Absent-mindedly he stared at the hands of his timepiece. At last he made up his mind about something and went inside the clapboard building that housed his offices.

'Jim, run down to the marshal's office and ask that new lawman to come up here.'

The errand boy ran the hundred yards to bring back the law officer.

The faint rumble of a vehicle could be heard. The manager peered hopefully up the road. A faint smudge of dust was just discernable in the direction from which the stage would be arriving. The depot manager was not sure if he should be grateful the stage was finally arriving or fearful of the consequences of its arrival. Marshal Horace Winterman arrived shortly before the stage hove in sight.

'Howdy,' he greeted the depot manager. 'Your boy said you wanted to see me.'

The manager glanced nervously at the group of men waiting for the arrival of the stage. 'Marshal, as you can see the stage is due. Those men, they're waiting for it. I'm worried they're up to no good.'

The marshal studied the men. 'You know any of them?'

'Just Mr Dane – the others are strangers to me.'

Horace's interest quickened. 'You did well to inform me. Did any of them buy a ticket?'

The manager shook his head.

Marshal Horace Winterman went inside the depot and kept watch from there. By then the stage was entering the town. The men he was watching straightened up and edged forward as the coach approached.

A thin cloud of dust drifted over the waiting men as the stage pulled to a halt. The depot manager strode forward trying not to show his nervousness.

'Elsinburg!' yelled the driver, as he hauled hard on the brakes. 'Half-hour break afore carrying on to Beckon Valley.'

The depot manager was opening the stagecoach door.

'Welcome, welcome to Elsinburg.'

A slim, clean-shaven youngster was first out. The lawman noted the gun belt underneath the jacket. The stranger spotted Clive Dane and stepped towards him. From the coach, three similarly attired young men stepped into the dust of the street and followed the first youngster. Clive Dane moved forward.

'Forten, I'm glad you could make it.'

As the two parties met, a cold feeling was worming its way inside Marshal Horace Winterman. He stayed where he was. The greetings completed, the nine men headed back up the street. Horace figured they were headed for the Cosmopolitan. Cautiously he followed.

Gertrude Dane sat in what had been Marian Lynas's bedroom. Her eyes felt gritty and there was a dull ache behind her eyes.

'Coffee and some breakfast might just perk me up,' she muttered.

Arriving late yesterday evening, the marshal had directed her to the Lynas house and her son. She had been surprised at the change in Russell. Her mind had been filled with images of a teenager – immature and moody. That boy existed no more. A man she hardly recognized had replaced her darling child. She had tried to embrace him and found herself holding a stiff awkward stranger.

Sighing at the fond memories that were all she had of a lost youngster, she stepped to the window and drew back the curtains. The thought of going downstairs and facing her son and the two strangers with him was daunting.

Leaning forward, the pressed her forehead against the glass hoping to get some relief from her throbbing headache. As she turned distractedly from the window her hand hit a small, carved, wooden box. It tumbled to the mat and spilled various items of jewellery.

'Damn.'

Gertrude allowed herself the luxury of a swearword as she bent to retrieve the box. A small, leather-bound book with the word diary embossed in gold nestled in the bottom. Gertrude stepped closer to the window for the better light and opened the journal. Some time lapsed before she emerged from her room.

Pausing at the head of the stairs she could hear voices from below. She put her hand up and pressed the palm of her hand against her eyes in an attempt to ease the intolerable tension.

'You gotta tell your ma.'

It was a woman's voice. The tension behind her eyes increased.

' 'Damnit, what am I to tell her – that her husband-to-be is a murderer?'

Gertrude swayed and put out her hand to grip the stair rail.

'It's not fair on her,' the female voice hissed. 'You do her and yourself an injustice withholding this information from her.'

Gertrude's head was light and had begun to spin. She thought she might fall down the stairs. She gripped tightly to the rail. Was she going mad? The intimate writings in the diary had dripped like a slow poison into her mind. Holding tightly to the rail she began the descent of the stairs.

Russell looked up as his mother came into the room. He took in her taut, pale face. The dark shadows beneath her eyes emphasized the anguish that was mirrored there.

'Mother, what is it?'

She held out the small leather book. 'This is Marian's diary. In it she logs details of the affair she had with

Charlie, your father.'

Seeing her standing there helplessly as if she were a little girl again and needing comforting broke down all reserves within him. Swiftly he crossed the room and folded her in his arms.

'Mother,' he murmured over and over again, his hand smoothing at her hair.

'But why, Russell? Is it really true? The assignations she lists correspond with things I remember happening – Charlie's buying trips and conventions.'

The tears flowed then. Behind his mother, Russell saw Peg hold up a mug and nod at his mother. He guided the weeping woman to the table and sat her down. Peg put the mug in front of her. Gertrude looked up at her son, her face a ruin of grief and pain.

'Was I such an awful wife, Russell?'

Russell sat and Peg put a mug in front of him. He shook his head. 'Ma, I understand none of it. I was as much shocked as you when I found out.'

'You knew!'

'Only after he was dead. Marian told me. That night when I killed Sheriff Lynas she lured me here for him to murder me.'

Her eyes were wide and staring at him.

'There is a more terrible thing you have to know, Mother.'

'Clive killed your father,' she said, before he could continue. 'It's all in the dairy. He ran the wagon over him to cover up. Sheriff Lynas helped. He found out about Marian and Charlie.'

Russell nodded slowly. 'Clive arranged to have me killed as well. Those two cowboys as were to take me to Texas were to make sure I did not return.'

'You knew about Clive and Lynas when you left? Why

148

didn't you tell me then?'

'Ma, I wasn't thinking straight. Clive had just rescued me from a lynching and was sending me to safety. I was confused. I ain't confused no more.' Russell wrapped his hands round his coffee mug as if drawing comfort from its warmth. 'Clive Dane is a dark horse all right. We found out he was a gunslinger down in Texas. Had a gang of gunnies he hired out to kill anyone as paid him. Things musta got too hot down there, for he returned here and I guess when he saw how well Pa had done for himself, he decided to kill him and take his place. Even down to marrying his widow.'

'Russell, don't. I know he wanted me, but I was so worried about you I couldn't think of marriage.'

She reached across the table and he took her small delicate hand in his.

36

'Russell, we got trouble.'

'What's up, Horace?'

'Clive Dane and Leonard Forten have teamed up together. They have a passel of gunnies with them. They've told the town they aim to finish this business once and for all, and afore the day's out they'll see you dead or hanged.'

Russell stared at his friend a few moments. 'Come inside, Horace.'

Horace glanced around the room at the people seated there. Gertrude Dane was sitting at the table looking lost and miserable. The formidable bulk of Peg was sprawled in a cushioned chair in one corner. Myron was standing by the window. He nodded to Horace and went back to studying the outside world.

'I guess they're right,' Russell remarked. 'This has got to end today.'

'Your horses are saddled and ready down at the livery. I've told the liveryman I'm gathering together a posse so as he don't suspect I'm trying to sneak you outta town.'

Russell was buckling on his gun. 'Thanks, Horace, you been a good friend.'

'Where will you go?'

'Me?' Russell shrugged. 'I'm going to the Cosmopolitan for a drink.'

Horace tried a smile. It was rather strained. 'No. I mean where will you go from here.'

Russell was spinning the cylinder on his Colt. Satisfied he dropped the weapon back in his holster.

'If I'm still alive after today, I guess I'll go back out to the ranch with Mother.'

'Russell, you don't understand. You can ride outta Elsinburg with me. By the time Forten and Clive realize what's happening, you'll be well outta the way.'

'Horace, Leonard Forten challenged me to a duel because my father killed his father. I ran away from that. My uncle killed my father and paid for hired guns to kill me. I ran away from that. I rode away from Elsinburg a boy. I've come back as a man. The man as come back doesn't run. He stands and fights.'

'Goddamn it, Russell, there's nine men out there looking for you. Each one of those men is a seasoned gunman capable of killing you without mercy. You go out in that street, you'll be dead afore you reach the Cosmopolitan.'

For answer Russell reached over and picked up the small diary. 'This will convict Clive of my father's murder.

150

Marian Lynas recorded it all in here. You take good care of this and use it to bring him to justice. In the meantime I gotta go and administer my own brand of justice.' He patted the butt of his holstered revolver.

Without opening it the lawman tucked the book inside his jacket.

'Raise your right hand.'

'What?' queried Russell, but he did as he was instructed.

'I'm swearing you in as deputy. We'll arrest that scheming sonabitch and see he hangs for murder. He's probably wanted for murder down in Texas as well.'

Russell was shaking his head. 'You can't do this, Horace. This is my fight.'

'Russell Dane, do you swear to uphold the laws of this country?'

'Goddamn it, Horace. . . .'

'Swear!'

'Damnit, I swear.'

'Lets go then.'

Out in the street the two men paused. Horace shaded his eyes and stared into the sky. 'Sure is a hot one, Hambone.'

Russell sighed. 'You know, that name is really beginning to rile me.'

'Don't worry, I'm sure your ma will put the right name on your tombstone.'

Russell looked out across the town. Just visible above the buildings was the cemetery. That was where it had all started. He had been a callow youth then, believing his father's spirit had come back to haunt the graveyard. Instead he had found Marian Lynas. It was as if some foul denizen from hell had been released and was intent on destroying all it came in contact with.

Since his father's murder, Sheriff Lynas and his wife

were dead. Rod Krantz and Gill Stern had tried to murder him and had died in the attempt. Elias Carter and Ichabod Goodyear lay buried in the hills somewhere.

The bullet still embedded in his chest seemed to move within him and suddenly he felt an immense power surge through him. He reached up and rubbed his chest where the scar of the bullet's entry was concealed beneath his shirt.

The spectre of death had cast its shadow across him so many times. This town had tried to lynch him and failed. His uncle's hired killers had tried also and he had survived. He had gone up against two vicious outlaws and lived to ride away. Suddenly he laughed out loud.

'You remember that story in the Bible, Horace, when Samson took a hambone and slaughtered loads of them there Philistines.'

Horace frowned at his young friend. Russell was grinning at him.

'Don't you see. All times I should have died and didn't. And the Hambone of God went down into Elsinburg and and killed himself a passel of Philistines.'

Russell's laughter was infectious. Horace found himself grinning back at his friend.

'If'n I remember it was the jawbone of an ass Samson used.'

'Hambone – jawbone – you think they'll know the difference?'

And suddenly they were both laughing. Two young men on their way to beard nine hardened killers with little hope of surviving and their mirth was perplexing. But it gave them both the strength and courage to walk on down into the town towards certain death.

'Hambone, was it mor'n nine Philistines that Samson killed?'

'I think it was a mite mor'n nine, Horace. I think he sent a thousand to meet their Maker that day.'

'A thousand you reckon. Mmm . . . well, we only got nine to take care of. Samson wouldn't have gotten out of bed for that many.'

Myron was watching the two friends.

'If that don't beat all! Hambone and his lawman friend are standing there, laughing fit to bust.' He shook his head. 'There's a town full of people just waiting to tear them fellas apart and they're laughing and joking as if they're on their way to a picnic. That Hambone, he's something else again.'

He heard movement in the room behind him and turned to see Peg pick up a shotgun. She hitched at her gun belt and moved towards the door.

'We riding out now, Peg?' he asked.

The big woman stared steadily back at him. 'I ain't riding nowheres till I see that there Hambone safe back with his mother.'

'It figgers. I guess I'll tag along with you.'

'Wait.'

They turned to see Gertrude Dane coming round the table toward them.

'I can shoot a gun as well, you know.'

Without a word, Peg handed her the shotgun.

37

'They're coming! The marshal and Dane are walking down the street in this direction.'

The noise in the Cosmopolitan hushed as the drinkers looked up at the breathless man in the doorway. He turned and peered back out into the street.

'Walking down here, cool as if they were on a Sunday school outing.'

Clive Dane looked over at Leonard Forten. They had sent their men into the town to seek out Russell. Others were down by the livery and at vantage points at other exits from the town. Their orders had been clear.

'You see that kid, you shoot to kill. Even if you don't get him with your first shots don't worry. We'll hear the firing and come running. If he's anywhere in this town we'll find him.'

Now the hunted man was coming to them. Forten smiled a thin, cold smile at the elder Dane.

'It couldn't be better. Leave him to me. He ran from me once. This time he won't get away.'

Dane nodded. 'Good, it's better this way. I can't have his blood on my hands. His ma wouldn't take kindly to marrying the man who gunned down her son. However, we'll need some insurance.' He signed to a man at a nearby table. 'Joe, round up the boys. Tell them the hare has come to the hounds.'

The man scuttled through the batwing doors. There was a sudden scramble as the drinkers vacated their seats and retreated to the interior of the bar-room. They wanted to be out of the line of flying lead, but they did not want to miss out on the action.

A silence descended on the Cosmopolitan. It was as if the saloon was holding its breath. The barkeep glanced over his shoulder at the gilt mirrors behind the bar and hoped they would be still intact when the shooting was over.

Leonard Forten ambled over to the bar. He hooked a foot in the brass rail running along the front. To those watching, he was the picture of coolness. He adjusted his gun belt and then slid his elbow onto the top of the bar. His other hand hung by his side and touched the polished walnut butt of his Peacemaker.

Clive Dane sat at a table smoking one of his cigars. Unseen, he slid out the pocket gun and held it beneath the table. He, too, looked cool and assured. The silence grew and the minutes ticked slowly by.

Outside the saloon, Horace silently gestured for Russell to wait. Cautiously he craned his neck and peered over the batwing doors. For a few moments he studied the interior before turning back to his companion.

'Forten is against the bar and your uncle is sitting at a table. We go in together, but keep a lookout for their gunmen. Maybe on the balcony or hid out back some-wheres.'

Russell stared back at his friend. 'Ready when you are, Horace.'

The friends stepped inside. No one spoke as they paused inside the doorway scanning the room for hidden gunnies. The men they had come to confront glared at the newcomers.

Russell eyed the two men before him and waited patiently. A supreme coolness possessed him. He watched for his enemies to make their move. It was Horace who broke the silence.

'Clive Dane, I am arresting you on suspicion of the murder of your brother, Charlie Dane.'

There was an audible gasp from the onlookers.

'I suppose my nephew cooked that one up to deflect attention from the murder of the Lynas family.'

'Nope, we have written testimony from Marian Lynas that you and her husband, Sheriff Paul Lynas, conspired

155

to murder Charlie Dane and pervert the course of justice by concealing the crime.'

Clive Dane gave a short disdainful laugh. 'Lies, all lies, Marshal. There's only one murderer in this room and he's standing right beside you.'

'Uncle Clive,' Russell greeted his uncle. 'I suppose you wonder why your pet coyotes didn't kill me as they were supposed to.'

Clive Dane drew deeply on his cigar.

'You remember Rod Krantz and Gill Stern – your paid killers? They're buried somewheres between here and Texas.'

Russell could see the barb sink home. His uncle's jaw tightened.

'Two more murders to add to your tally. You sure took after your father. He always was a no-good womanizer and killer.'

'The hell with this nonsense,' the young man at the bar interrupted. 'Your yellow-belly nephew and me has some unfinished business.'

Horace never took his eyes from the man sitting at the table as Forten called out his insult. Russell stepped clear of the marshal.

'Forten, I have no quarrel with you. My father wronged your family. I know that now. I can't make it right but I don't want to fight with you. We can shake hands and walk away from this.'

The smile on Leonard Forten's face was wide and cynical. 'Yellow – just like I had you figured.' He stepped away from the bar, his hand a claw above the handle of his Peacemaker. 'You ran away from me once, Dane. I ain't giving you the chance to get away this time. I intend to kill you. I tell you now you won't make it out that door when you turn tail and run for it.'

'So be it,' Russell said softly, and waited for his challenger to make his move.

The seconds dragged. No one in the saloon dared to move. Some men feared to blink in case they missed anything.

Horace stood beside his friend. All the time he was watching Clive Dane sitting at his table and smoking calmly.

'Die, Dane!' snarled Leonard Forten and snatched at the butt of his Peacemaker.

Russell's Colt leapt into his hand and he triggered his shot at the man who was so eager to kill him. Forten's pistol had not cleared the holster when the shot hit him high in the chest. He staggered back, a look of shock and surprise on his face. He was staring at the youth he had called yellow. Slowly, as if a great weariness overwhelmed him, he sank to the floor, his weapon forgotten with the great pain exploding in his chest. He opened his mouth to speak but suddenly his body went limp and he keeled over backwards.

When the shot from Russell's gun blasted out, Horace made the mistake of taking his eye off Clive Dane. He did not see the gun come up from under the table. Clive Dane was aiming at his nephew. The small calibre pocket-gun was notoriously inaccurate even at these short distances. The first bullet hit Horace in the chest. He was punched back and tumbled to the floor.

Russell's reaction was instinctive. He was watching with some anguish his fallen opponent, when the flash and bang of the pistol swung him round. He hardly registered the man firing the weapon. A bullet stung his arm. Again he triggered.

Seeing him come round, Clive flung himself to the floor behind the table. As he fell he was pulling out his holstered Colt. He had favoured the hideout gun because of its stealth. Now he needed firepower and accuracy, so he pulled his Colt.

From his position on the floor he could only see Russell's lower body. This time his shot was fast and accurate. Russell felt a mighty blow on his thigh. He spun round and grabbed at the bar to keep upright. In doing so, he lost his grip on his Colt. Clive Dane saw the weapon fall to the floor. Slowly he stood – his pistol aimed at his nephew.

'Goddamn you, Russell, why can't you stay dead? The lynching was supposed to take care of you. Then Rod Krantz and Gill Stern botched the job. There's a saying that if you want a job doing you gotta do it yourself.' Clive Dane smiled thinly. 'Time to join your pa. Give him my best regards. Tell him I'll be enjoying his widow.'

'The widow says, no more!'

Clive Dane turned his shocked gaze towards the voice. Framed in the doorway was a woman. She was trembling with fear and emotion. The shotgun in her hands was pointed steadily in the direction of her brother-in-law.

'Gertrude, I never meant—'

Clive Dane swivelled and shot his brother's widow. Gertrude Dane was punched back into the doors. The shotgun in her hands tumbled to the floor.

'No!'

Russell was screaming as he flung himself towards his uncle. The distance was too great. He could not beat a bullet, but he tried anyway. Russell's leg gave way beneath him. The shot blasted out and went over his head as he fell. Another shot came and Russell was clawing his way across the floor towards his uncle. He looked up expecting the next shot to punch him back into the sawdust. He stopped moving.

Clive Dane staggered back, a red hole blossoming in his throat. The gun in his hand was pointing towards the floor. Russell stared at the wounded man, bewildered at the sudden turn of events. There was movement beside him and he turned to meet the new attacker.

Horace Winterman was standing with a smoking pistol in his hand waiting for Clive Dane to fall. There was the thud of a body hitting the floorboards, and Clive Dane twitched out his life in the sawdust of the Cosmopolitan Saloon.

'Horace, I thought you was dead.'

The lawman grimaced and pulled a small leather-bound book from an inside pocket. A hole had been punched in the leather and a piece of misshapen lead fell to the floor.

'Hurts like hell, but it sure stopped Clive's goddamn bullet.'

Russell's face suddenly clouded over.

'Mother.'

He tried to get to his feet but his wounded leg would not support him. He felt Horace's strong arm around him and he hobbled to the door. Gertrude Dane lay sprawled on the boardwalk. Peg and Myron were standing with drawn guns trained on half a dozen gunmen lined up in the street. Setting Russell down beside the body of his mother, Horace stepped forward.

'I'm Marshal Horace Winterman. Leonard Forten and Clive Dane are both dead. I advise you to get out of town. Come sundown, if I see any of you still around I'll arrest you.'

There was no argument. Without a word the men turned and walked away.

Russell was cradling the body of his mother in his arms. His tears dripped onto her dead face. Horace gripped his shoulder.

'Russell, we gotta get that leg seen to. I'll look after your mother.' The lawman looked up at Peg. 'You two get him down to the sawbones.'

*

'Come, Hambone, it's over now.'

'This is where it all started, Peg, and this is where it ends.'

The mourners were dispersing back down the cemetery hill.

'Your mother is at rest now beside her husband. I'll help you down to the carriage.'

Russell twisted round on his crutches and with Peg on one side and Myron on the other he hobbled from the Dane sepulchre.